From Glasgow Without Love

'A racy collection of stories captivating and relatable in almost equal measures served in riveting prose with the power to keep readers yearning for more.'

Olukorede Yishau, *Author*

'Albrin Junior is a witty, stylish and always surprising writer. His story 'Deceived' is a tale of romance, intrigue, and revelations to rival any Shakespearean play. What a treat!'

Dr Carly Brown, *Author*.

'From Glasgow Without Love is an engrossing collection of stories that adamantly depicts the elemental misfortune of being human, done in the offhanded manner which typifies Albrin's story telling behaviour.'

Ray Anyasi, *Author*

'This book creates a series of stories that covers an important spectrum of issues, all, I think relevant and timely. Through all of them there runs a humanistic spirit, sometimes subtly expressed, but even in the texts that touch on the spiritual or mystical notions, I never lost sight of the humanity of the characters drafted. Short story writing is a particular art. Albrin captured in most of these a complex range of emotions and reactions. The writing is quite strong – clear, clever where it needs to be, intense when necessary, and accessible. I applaud your ability to create dialogue that is both realistic and informative in developing the characters. I like this collection very much.'

Greg Fields, *Author. Editor*

'This new collection of stories by Albrin Junior takes us deep into the heart of the human condition. As we move between the United Kingdom and Nigeria, love and desperation walk hand in hand. Albrin peels back the layers of his characters so that we understand that they are complex and nuanced, made vulnerable by their struggles – sometimes with tragic results. Throughout, there is keen eye for observation, and an ability to imbue the highest of drama with notes of hope for a better future. Albrin Junior is an important new voice in contemporary fiction.'

Dr Zoë Strachan, *Professor of Creative & Interdisciplinary Practise*

First published 2024

Copyright © Albrin Junior 2024

The right of Albrin Junior to be identified as the author of this work has been asserted in accordance with the Copyright, Designs & Patents Act 1988.

All rights reserved. No part of this book may be reproduced, stored in a retrieval system, or transmitted in any form or by any means, digital, electronic, electrostatic, magnetic tape, mechanical, photocopying, recording or otherwise, without the written permission of the copyright holder.

Published under licence by Brown Dog Books and
The Self-Publishing Partnership Ltd, 10b Greenway Farm, Bath Rd,
Wick, nr. Bath BS30 5RL, UK

www.selfpublishingpartnership.co.uk

ISBN printed book: 978-1-83952-876-7
ISBN e-book: 978-1-83952-877-4

Cover design by Kevin Rylands
Internal design by Andrew Easton

Printed and bound in the UK

This book is printed on FSC® certified paper

From Glasgow Without Love
A collection beyond fiction

Albrin Junior

BROWN DOG BOOKS

For

TALABI SAMUEL

Alas! How unchivalrous death is.

If only he were kind and chanced you,

to see that which we often talked about;

Writing tales that men crave.

Stories

1	From Glasgow Without Love	11
2	One Gay Night	27
3	Fake London Girl	63
4	Love in a Time of Massacre	85
5	Deceived	103
6	Diary of a Black Immigrant	117
7	The Devil Has a Soul	149
8	Unshaped Gold	167
9	Drown	191
10	Even gods Cry	239

FROM GLASGOW WITHOUT LOVE

If you're willing and obedient, you shall eat the good of the land;
but if you refuse and rebel,
you shall be devoured by the sword;
for the mouth of the lord has spoken.

Isaiah 1:19-20

'We are about to close, sir.'

Elvis swivelled back to see the docent of Kelvingrove Art and Gallery Museum standing over his shoulder with a broad smile.

'Thank you,' he nodded, and she walked away.

Since Molly got pregnant, he dreaded returning home at night. The setting sun was a reminder of the potential horror he would have to endure, and every night was a different kind of drama she often blamed on hormonal imbalance. 'Like you're the first person to ever be pregnant!' he usually grumbled beneath his breath.

Elvis waited until the last person left the building before standing to leave. He flashed a smile to the docent as he walked past her while holding on to the tip of his cap.

'Aye, he's a gentleman now,' said the security man to the docent. 'Why d'ye think he stays here so late?'

'Scared tae go hame,' she replied, and shifted her gaze to Elvis as he walked down the stairs. 'Probably got a naggin' missus waitin' fer him wi a fryin' pan.'

'Aye! I feel for him but I think mine's shittier. I'll be goin' hame to some charcoal tea.'

They both burst into laughter.

Elvis turned back, casting a long, sad gaze at the museum and saw the pair laughing. They stopped at once, waved at Elvis and feigned a smile. Elvis managed to wave back, wondering what about him had made them laugh.

He looked at his wristwatch; it was a little after 5pm. He shook his head and thought to go and sit at the Kelvingrove's café but remembered coming across Molly's best friend, Emily, the last time he was there. When Molly questioned what he was doing there when his shift had ended and he was supposed to be home, he'd lied and said he was with his boss.

He got into his car and drove down Paisley West Road to Cardonald, stopping to park in front of Castles, a small independent restaurant that served both classic and contemporary dishes. The place was small and cosy, simple and welcoming just as its owner and chef, David. Elvis had worked there as a kitchen porter when he first moved to Glasgow after absconding from Birmingham. When he had arrived in the United Kingdom, the restaurant was the first place he was treated like a human being and not seen as Black.

'Elvis!' David exclaimed as Elvis walked in, 'All right!' He bumped his fist in a spirited fashion.

'It's me in the flesh,' said Elvis, feigning enthusiasm.

'I can see that! Just give me a few minutes. Let me do something in the kitchen.' He turned to a waiter and said, 'Serve him anything he wants. It's on the house.'

The waiter approached Elvis, who sat now at the far end of the restaurant away from prying eyes. Three months of working in the kitchen and he still couldn't name any of their dishes, except for Collin's Italian Spaghetti. His mind was, however, too preoccupied for him to eat.

'A martini would do,' said Elvis to the waiter. 'Thank you.'

He shifted his gaze to the sign carved against the wall, grey and lit, its elegance adding beauty to the feel of the restaurant. His drink arrived just as David returned to sit with him.

'Yo my man, what's up?' David asked.

Elvis stared at David contemplating whether to tell the truth or reply with a lie which had become a common response: 'Fine'. He feared if he spoke the truth, the wind would blow his whispers to Molly's ears and everything for him would be over. Molly was his last hope at cementing a better life or at least what would appear to be a better life compared to where he came from.

'I'm fine.' He feigned a grin.

'All right!' David nodded. 'And Molly? How're she and the baby coming?'

'Fine,' Elvis responded in a low tone, then without warning, he burst into silent tears. 'I am not fine, David. I am in deep shit.'

'Fuck! What's wrong? Talk to me.'

'I don't even know where to begin.'

'Anywhere, mate, anywhere.' David leaned forward.

Elvis sniffed, mulling over the words to use to tell the man sitting opposite him that he was an illegal immigrant and his love for Molly was conditional. He heaved a deep sigh and gulped down his martini for some form of courage but found none at the end of the glass.

'Talk to me my friend.'

Elvis looked into the glass it was empty. He needed more than courage to tell David he was in this situation as a result of his own stupidity, an eagerness to make quick money.

'This thing, whatever it is, does Molly know?' asked David, killing the silence.

Elvis's phone rang. It was Molly. He silenced the phone with urgency and cursed under his breath. 'Shit!' He looked around for any familiar faces then back to David, who was staring at him in bewilderment.

'Are you okay?'

'No. Yes. I got to go.'

Elvis rose and started away, leaving David agape.

In less than fifteen minutes Elvis was at Hillhead unlocking the door to his house. He walked in to find Molly sitting on the couch in silence, which he thought was odd considering her routinely welcoming him with screams and questions about his lateness and whereabouts.

'Hey babe.' He made to kiss her protruding stomach but she shoved his face away. 'Are you okay?'

Molly folded her arm and looked away. Her countenance since Elvis arrived had been unpleasant. He followed her eyes and noticed his travel bag was laid on the couch and his belongings scattered all over the sitting room.

'What is going on?' Elvis asked.

'Is there something you want to tell me?' Molly asked.

Elvis winced. 'Shit!' he exclaimed beneath his breath as he ran for the bag. '*The letter!*' He dived into the bag hurling the remains of his belongings out until he reached the bottom, shaking the bag for something to fall out. He set it down looking terrified.

'Looking for this?' said Molly behind him.

He turned around and saw a familiar envelope on the centre table. 'Fuck!' he mouthed.

'Yes. You're fucked.'

'Babe – I know you're mad, but let me explain.'

'Explain what?' she scoffed. 'You don't even know what's in the letter.'

Elvis opened his mouth to talk but found the words wouldn't come out.

'Go ahead,' Molly said, 'read it. I would love to know what the letter says.'

'Babe, I don't need to…'

'I said read the damn fucking letter,' she shouted, making a fist. Elvis nodded. 'I'm trying hard not to disturb the baby,' she said rubbing her stomach. 'So please just read the damn fucking letter.'

Elvis picked up the letter and cleared his throat. He looked at Molly hoping she'd have a change of mind but the anger on her face suggested otherwise.

'Dear Elvis Osahon,' he began. 'This is to inform you that…'

'Won't you at least let me know who it is from?'

Elvis scowled, concealing his distress.

'UKVI.' The tone of his voice was losing strength. Molly nodded and urged him on. 'This is to inform you that we have withdrawn your right to live and work in the United Kingdom…'

Elvis paused as those words flushed his memory with recollected thoughts of how he could have avoided this letter, avoided Molly. He continued the letter. 'This is as a result of the University of Birmingham informing us of withdrawing your admission offer due to lack of attendance and tuition payment. You are hereby advised to…' Elvis stopped reading and slid the letter into his pocket. 'Babe, let me explain.'

Molly's face was livid. 'You know I crosschecked the date the letter was sent. Isn't it funny that we moved to Glasgow just weeks after that, and all of a sudden you declared you wanted to have a baby with me?'

'Molly, you also said you wanted a baby.'

'No!' Molly shouted getting to her feet. 'Don't even go there, Elvis. Don't!'

'The same want, just different reasons,' said Elvis beneath his breath.

'But you want a child with me to secure your stay in this country.'

'No,' Elvis said, shaking his head with impatience. 'You're an erratic junkie no white man wants anything to do with. You chose me because I am Black and can be used,' he retorted, 'and if we're being fair, you started using me before this letter ever arrived.'

She struck his face so hard it sent a wave of shock down Elvis's spine. He paused a few seconds, holding his face, and when he lifted it, his right eye was red.

'I know you're mad, but please can we just talk this out without cursing and fighting?'

'You lying bastard,' Molly hit him over and over again. As he stood allowing her to vent without impeding her punches, he closed his eyes, disappointed that his secret was finally out and unsure what would happen next. With Molly, he wasn't sure of anything. Her reactions made him feel worse than a cheating husband, like he had betrayed the very core of their relationship, yet in his guilt, he knew they had both betrayed each other Regardless of her fitful nature, he was sure she loved him, and he loved her, he always did – in a complicated way – until the letter from UKVI came. Then his love for her became selfish. He became focused on remaining in a land in which he was never welcomed in the first place.

'Molly, please. Just stop. You're hurting yourself and the baby.'

'Baby!' Molly exclaimed then burst into sudden capricious laughter. 'You no longer have a baby.'

'Molly,' Elvis said with a sense of impending danger. 'Whatever it is you're thinking, don't.'

Molly looked over Elvis's shoulder with a humourless smile. Following her eyes, Elvis swivelled. She was staring at the kitchen. She made an attempt to run into the kitchen but he blocked her path.

'Molly, whatever it is, don't do it. Please, I beg you.'

'It's too late for that,' she yelled, trying to circle round him. She made a run for it but he grabbed her and she yelled in pain.

'The baby, the baby!'

Elvis set her free, attempting to rub her stomach from worry when she hit him hard on the face and dashed for the kitchen, ripping part of his shirt in the process. He was still tending to his face when she returned with a knife.

'Babe. Why are you holding a knife?'

'Is it this baby you speak of?' she said, lifting the knife to her stomach, poised to drive it in. 'You won't have it. We won't give you the pleasure of using us to remain in this country. Go back to where you came from, Monkey.'

'Molly, think about this. You'll hurt yourself too.'

'I don't care.'

She lifted the knife, about to drive it down, when Elvis shouted.

'Okay, okay, okay. Fine, I will leave. Just don't do anything to hurt the baby.'

'Just leave and never come back.'

'Yeah. Yeah. At least let me get my stuffs?'

Molly looked down at his scattered bag and clothes and nodded. Elvis bent to gather his things, and in one moment of Molly looking away, he leapt at her, grabbing the knife but cutting her arm as he overpowered her.

'My hand!' Molly screamed. 'You fucking bastard! You want to kill me!'

'It was a mistake, I swear it.'

'You're not getting away with this.'

Molly grabbed her phone, dialled a number and held the phone to her ear.

'Who are you calling?' Elvis asked.

'What do you think?' Molly replied without looking at him.

'Molly, drop the phone. You know my life will be over when they get here.'

'I don't care,' Molly said with a broad malevolent beam. 'Hello,' she said into the phone. 'I have a crime to report. My partner just tried to kill me—'

'Shit!' Elvis cursed, looking about in disarray. He shifted his gaze to the car key on the table beside Molly, then ran out the house with the knife in his hands.

Elvis sat alone in the busy concourse of the Buchanan bus station as the world around him moved in a hurry whilst his crashed down. Staring long at the wincher's statue, he thought back to the beginning of the decline of his life, which began at age sixteen back in Nigeria: when his mother could no longer give him pocket money for school, when he didn't read along with his classmates because he could not afford to buy the class text, when he had to carry a tray along the minor arterial highway after school to sell bread so he and his mother could eat. He was amazed the day Bashiru, their neighbour's son who had left five months ago, returned home driving a tear-rubber Camry. He couldn't help but wonder why

Bashiru's parents, who claimed not to know his whereabouts, didn't scold him. Instead, along with other neighbours, they dashed out praising his accomplishment at such a young age, and collectively prayed his business would continue to thrive so he could change his parents' lives for good.

'What business are you into?' Elvis had asked Bashiru after the charade came to an end.

'The business of being smart and fast,' he replied.

'And in five months you bought a car?!' Elvis exclaimed. 'Introduce me to your business.'

Bashiru laughed. He looked at Elvis from head to toe and could feel his aura of ambition. 'If you say so. Have you heard of yahoo yahoo?'

'Yahoo yahoo!' Elvis reiterated in awe. 'What is that?'

Bashiru laughed at Elvis's innocence.

'Take a walk with me and I will tell you everything you need to know,' he said.

Six months later, Elvis bought his own car, renovated their old house and put his mother on a monthly salary. A couple of years later after the success of his yahoo-yahoo ventures began to dwindle, he gathered the remains to sponsor himself to study in the United Kingdom with the believe it would be a greener pasture, promising his mother before he departed that he would make her proud. He arrived in Birmingham to find the green pasture wasn't so green, and that his yahoo enterprise could not thrive, a realisation that came after he had squandered the little money he had. 'School is not for me, I need to make money,' Elvis had convinced himself.

'Hey, you okay, mate?' a security guard in a reflective jacket nudged Elvis out of his thoughts. 'You look lost,' the guard said.

Elvis feigned a smile and shook his head. 'Thank you, I am fine.'

He watched the guard move back to his post, leaving him to his loneliness. He returned his gaze to the wincher's statue, trying to imagine the story behind the sculpture. He found himself thinking about his mother and home. There was no home to go back to, nor was there one to look forward to; he had come to terms with his fate. The fault was not in his stars but in himself. He thought to close his eyes and whisper a prayer to God; perhaps, God in his mercies would come to his aid, but on a second thought, he reckoned his remedy –which he wanted to ascribe to heaven – lay in himself.

Rather than let his story end in the ink of another, Elvis decided he would write his own ending in his own ink with the hope that his story would not merely headline the Metro to sell the papers, but deter others from making his mistakes. All may not have been well for him, but all would end well.

He brought out his phone and typed.

'Sorry how things turned out, would have wished it differently. I did love you from the start, maybe complicated, but love you I did. Till we meet again.'

After a minute of indecision, he sent the text to Molly. He took one last look around the concourse, then closed his eyes to inhale the cold air of the night. He removed the knife from his pocket and started for the centre of the space.

'He's got a knife,' some woman shouted, pointing at Elvis.

Elvis quickly grabbed the woman beside him who was attempting to run in the other direction. He put the knife to her neck.

'Just do what I say and I won't hurt you,' Elvis told her. She nodded in terror, and lifted her hands in surrender. 'Keep moving till I say stop.' The woman obeyed. 'Stop,' he told her on reaching the centre.

In a matter of seconds, the concourse was nearly empty except for onlookers in the distance capturing the scene with their phones. The security guards stood in disarray contemplating their next action.

'Stay where you are or I will hurt her.' Elvis raised his voice at the guards, and then whispered to the woman, 'That is an empty threat. Don't be afraid.'

The woman gulped saliva. It was hard to believe a man with a knife to her throat.

'Please don't hurt me,' pleaded the woman in a shaky voice.

'I won't, I promise.' Elvis took the knife off her throat. 'You can put your hands down,' he told her.

The woman nodded and obeyed, slowly. She took a look around the concourse. All eyes were on her and Elvis. She gulped again, took a quick peek at the security guards then shifted her gaze back to Elvis. 'Will you let me go then?'

Elvis shook his head.

The woman sniffed her silent tears. 'Why are you doing this?'

'Do you have kids?' he asked her.

'Yes,' she answered, concealing the terror in her voice. 'Just one.'

'And are you proud of him? Or her?'

'Him,' she nodded. 'Yes, I am proud.'

Elvis let out a wide grin. 'I have one too. Technically still on the way,' he forced a laugh. 'But I swear I love him, or her. Even though I did it for a selfish reason.' Elvis put his hand over his face in an attempt not to cry.

From the corner of her eye, the woman saw one of the security guards signalling at her to make a run for it. She shook her head slightly, swallowed, and returned her face to Elvis.

'I fucked up,' said Elvis, in between his tears. 'I really fucked up.'

The woman looked closer at him. She saw the sadness in his eyes, the puddle of tears hidden behind his corneas.

'You still have time to make corrections.'

Elvis shook his head. 'That boat already sailed.' He burst into tears and placed his head on the woman's shoulder. 'Do you think my mother will be proud of me after she sees this?'

The woman searched his eyes, she saw he was broken and sincere. 'A mother will always be proud of her children regardless of their actions.'

Two police officers arrived pointing their guns at him while the guards kept the onlookers at bay.

Elvis turned the woman to the police and held his knife firmly to her neck.

'We have you surrounded,' said an officer. 'Put the knife down and kneel.'

Elvis ignored him and whispered to the woman. 'At my signal, you break free and run left. Do you understand me?'

The woman nodded, her dread having returned.

'What direction?' he asked the woman. She made to point but he stopped her. 'Stop,' he tapped her. 'Just move your head that way if you understand.'

The woman turned her head to the left and back.

'Good,' said Elvis. 'Now run.'

The woman broke free from his grip and ran to her left.

Elvis smiled and swivelled to the officer who shouted, 'Down on your knees!'

Elvis took a step towards the officer, who without hesitation fired one shot to his arm, then another to his chest. The knife fell, then Elvis fell. And just before he hit the ground, he imagined hearing the untamed cry of a toddler. He landed facing the wincher's statue with a smile. In that moment, he pictured himself arriving home, his travel bag landing on the floor as his mother ran into his open arms. Little by little, the life in his eye departed. Nothing in his life became him like the leaving of it.

ONE GAY NIGHT

Meredith Galloway held a knife to her throat while staring at her reflection in the mirror. After a few minute of firm contemplation, she let go of the knife and fell to the ground in near tears. This was her fifteenth attempt at suicide since she had been put through the foster-care system, but each time she tried, she was dissuaded by two things; the hope that the life ahead of her could be better than the one she had left behind, and that only cowards take their own life. She wasn't a coward. Her phone began to beep repeatedly. She picked it up; it was an alarm set for 23:00. *Club tonight*, was the inscription on the screen.

She heaved a sigh and wiped her tears. Picked herself back up and kicked the knife with disdain. She took off her black contrast lace top, revealing her bare back, and her East West breasts swung freely both ways. Scattered about her back from her shoulder to her waist were red sore marks of strokes and piercing fingers.

Her phone rang. She looked up the caller. It was a number she knew only too well – her mother. She ended the call, staring at the phone with ambivalence when a text popped up.

Please Meredith. Pick up.

Meredith hissed through her teeth and started for the bathroom in her white pants— except for the side the pant covered in brown contour lines. As the broiling water from the shower rained down on her head through to her feet, the text from her mother flashed through her mind, and it made her all the more upset. She often wondered who she hated more between her mother and the government; her mother for not fighting for her, or the government who took her from her mother. The government and her mother were the reason she had turned out the way she had; and she was never going to forgive them. Howbeit, deep down she cried in secret, knowing the fault began with her.

Meredith walked out of the bathroom naked, with only a towel around her head. She looked pale and thin, with sore marks on almost every part of her body. Each mark told a story, stories that haunted her long after she had lived them. She let loose the towel, and her full long blonde hair – which touched the back of her waist– tumbled down. She checked the time on her phone, it was 10:35pm, and was about to request a ride when the same number as earlier began calling.

'For God's sake, Mum!' Meredith mouthed with a frown.

She stared at the phone till the call ended then requested a ride. She returned to towel- drying her hair when her phone beeped, and a text message from the same number popped up.

I am sorry. I should have fought for you.

Meredith read the message. She was quiet for a few seconds. She bent her knee and held it to her face as the memory of that haunting sunny afternoon flooded her. She was ten years of age when social services came to take her. The tall female social worker stretched out her hand to Meredith and said, 'You will be fine with us. We will take you to a family where you can be who you want to be.' Meredith smiled, grabbed her bags and walked with the woman out the door as she watched her mother shed helpless tears. At the time, Meredith was too young to know her mother was helpless, but now that she knew better, she had blamed her mother long enough not to want to admit that there was nothing her mother could have done.

Her phone rang.

'Hello,' she answered.

'You ordered an Uber. I am outside your apartment.'

'Shit!'

Meredith jumped off the bed and into a black crop top and a blue crazy-jean bum-short.

Half an hour later, Meredith was outside the Uptown Club, and catwalked past the queue to the entrance.

'Hey gorgeous,' said the bouncer to Meredith. 'Will tonight be my lucky night to tap that?' he asked, staring at her with lust.

'Not tonight,' Meredith replied heartily.

They laughed and he let her into the club. Behind her, she heard some people in the queue murmur about unfairness and inequality.

Meredith nodded her head through the crowd. The music in the club was loud and electric.

'Smirnoff vodka,' she said to the man behind the counter.

'Dancing tonight?' the barman asked.

Meredith looked back to the dance floor; it was covered with red and blue strobe lights and sweaty hands dangling in the air.

'The night is still young,' she replied.

The drink came and Meredith sipped slowly. The club and alcohol was how she forgot about her past, and it worked every other night she went clubbing, but on the nights she stayed home sober, she cried her eyes out.

'Whisky please,' came a female voice from behind.

Meredith turned to the woman who was about to sit beside her. She was dressed in a gold satin ruched side-slip mini dress, but in a sexually rebellious way. Her hair was ebony-black and it flowed over her shoulders, complementing her thin white skin in a jaw-dropping manner.

The woman turned to Meredith and flashed her a smile. Her beguiling white teeth lit up the club, but what sent electric waves through Meredith were the woman's cherry-sweet lips which looked soft pressed against the glass of whisky in her hand.

'Hi,' the woman said over the music, making a slight nod at Meredith.

Meredith froze, and caught her breath for a moment. She looked behind her; there was no one there. She composed herself and smiled back.

'Hi,' Meredith replied. She struggled with what to say next, and after a few seconds found herself saying, 'Your teeth, are they dental implants?'

'I can't hear you,' the woman placed her hand behind her ear.

'I asked if your teeth are dental implants?' Meredith shouted over the music.

The woman giggled then let out a smile revealing the lower part of her teeth. 'No, all natural,' she replied.

Meredith nodded, impressed, unable to take her eyes away from the woman. She had a comely figure which was stem-thin, and a thin white skin of unblemished hue.

'Can I tell you something?' the woman said to Meredith. Meredith nodded. The woman leaned forward and whispered in a solemn titillating voice, 'You're pretty. Makes it hard to take my eyes off you.'

Meredith sat still and in awe. She didn't know what to feel, or how to feel what she felt. It had been four years since she clocked eighteen and came out of the foster-care system, and this was the first time anyone had made her feel the way she felt. She had come to the same club, sat on the same seat and drank the same drink these last four years hoping someone, just anyone, would find her attractive enough to make sexual advances, and now that it was happening, she was all too confused and ecstatic at the same time.

'Thank you,' Meredith replied coyly. 'You're prettier.'

'I didn't hear you,' said the woman as she leaned towards Meredith.

'I said you're prettier.'

'Thank you,' the woman blushed, and placed her hand on Meredith's thigh.

Meredith felt a cold exhilarating sensation tingle down her spine. The woman let her varnished fingernails hover over Meredith's lap then slowly dragged them away. Meredith closed her thighs in a thrill of ecstasy. The woman leaned back, flashed a consummate grin, and Meredith couldn't tell exactly what it meant, but what she knew was that she was being led on and she loved every bit of it.

'You are not a regular here,' said Meredith, breaking the silence.

'Are you?' asked the woman.

Meredith nodded, and found that she wanted to tell the woman everything she knew about the club, and to her greatest surprise, about herself too. Somehow, she felt some sort of ease and comfort in sharing her life's tale with a stranger knowing no form of self-righteousness and judgement might arise.

The song, 'messy in heaven' by Venbee, echoed through the speakers of the club and Meredith shot to her feet.

'I love this song,' said Meredith at the top of her voice.

'It's hard to hear you. The music is loud,' the woman said to Meredith.

'You should let this song go through you.'

Meredith wriggled to the dance floor while watching the woman sip her drink and stare at her with lust. Meredith was electric, she moved around the dance floor with flawless steps, dancing with a man, and with a woman, then on her own, and for every one of those moments, she stole glances at the woman, and knew what came next, or what most likely would.

Meredith approached the woman.

'Join me on the dance floor,' she said at the top of her voice.

The woman shook her head with a smile.

'I am not a dancer.'

'I can teach you.'

The crowd cheered aloud as the DJ switched to another song.

'I said I can teach you.'

'I'm bored. You want to do something else?' the woman countered.

'What do you have in mind?'

'Smoke.'

Meredith stared at the woman with interest and nodded. 'Okay.'

The woman finished her drink and waved to the barman with a debit card in her palm. The barman input an amount into the till and she swiped her card.

'It didn't go through,' the barman said, showing her the device.

'What do we do?' the woman asked.

'You can transfer into that account number.' The barman pointed to the account number taped to the bar. 'The machine will generate a receipt for you.'

A few seconds later, after touching her phone, the woman nodded to the barman, 'Done,' then turned to Meredith and said, 'Let's go.' She tucked her phone into her handbag and started for the exit.

The paper receipt slid out of the machine. The barman waved it to the woman but she was already gone.

'I will take it to her,' said Meredith to the barman. She grabbed the receipt and went after the woman.

Meredith stepped outside to see the woman lighting a smoke. She inhaled and puffed a great amount in sheer delight, and Meredith couldn't be more enchanted watching her.

'You smoke?' she asked Meredith.

'Not really. Sometimes.'

The woman placed a cigar in Meredith's mouth, then lit it. Meredith inhaled, and coughed. The woman smiled.

'Why?' the woman asked in between her smokes.

'Hmm! Why what?'

'I've never understood the concept behind clubbing. Why waste so much money and energy for a fleeting pleasure?'

'Several reasons I guess,' Meredith puffed. 'To blow off steam. To dance and get high with other people. To try to forget something. To try to get laid.'

The woman stepped on her cigar, and flashed Meredith a lusty gaze.

'Is that what you want?' she asked, 'To get laid?'

Meredith was about to say something when the woman leaned forward and kissed her, deep. A few seconds later, just as Meredith was about to get into the kiss, the woman pulled away.

The kiss lingered on Meredith's lips, and her body shuddered, sending shock waves stirring through her skin. Her bones vibrated. She touched her lips and stared at the woman, bowled over. For as long as she could remember, this was the first kiss she had received that wasn't imposed, and it tasted different. It tasted genuine and gave a sense of connection unlike any she had never felt before. It awoke in her a different kind of longing which she wasn't aware she had, and she didn't care if it was a man or woman making her feel the way she felt, she loved it, and didn't want it to end.

'I don't even know your name,' Meredith said after a long, ambivalent silence.

'I could tell you,' the woman said, with a hint of sexuality in her voice, 'but is that what you really want to know?' 'What is in a name, when my lips could taste as sweet.'

Meredith gulped. The woman kissed her again. This time, Meredith gave way for the woman's tongue to roam free inside her mouth. The woman grabbed Meredith below her waist and pressed their breasts against each other.

Meredith pulled back.

'Are you sure about this? Why me? Do you love me?' Meredith asked.

'Do you always ask this many questions?' replied the woman.

She pulled Meredith closer with her leg, kissed her nape, and Meredith moaned to the sky.

'Let's go to your place,' the woman kissed Meredith's nape.

'Are you sure?' Meredith asked in a doubtful tone, but her eyes suggested it was what she yearned for.

'Only if you want,' the woman replied.

'Yes,' responded Meredith. 'I will order a taxi.'

Every so often at night now, Meredith dreamt about the best times of her life, which were from the age she could remember to the age of ten, and in those dreams, she often found herself dreaming about living those moments again in the present. But every so often, she woke to realise she was within the four walls of her quaint, shoddy room, and the scars on her back that pressed against the single spring bed she lay on reminded her of the life she had endured since she was ten.

Last night wasn't one of those nights for Meredith because her dream was laden with the thrills of a sexual encounter, and when dawn came, she was woken by the buzz of her phone. She opened her eyes unwillingly and let out a lazy yawn. She reached for her phone; it showed four missed calls and a text which read:

Where you at? Boss is pissed off.

'Shit!' Meredith murmured and dropped the phone.

'Hey babe,' said Meredith as she turned to her side. 'Good morn—', she wanted to say, but to her surprise, there was no one there. She lifted her head and looked around, but it was just her within the paint-peeling walls of her room.

Meredith opened her mouth to call out the woman's name, then realised she didn't know her name. She stared at the poorly mixed red-yellow walls of her room, muddled. It was like yesterday didn't happen, like she made up the events of last night. But Meredith was sure she went clubbing at Uptown, met a beautiful stunning woman, and they both ended up at her place and made out. With the woman, Meredith felt seen, heard, and loved. It may not have been love at first sight, but it was close to it, and she had the impression that it was genuine – like she was special, but now, she wasn't sure anymore.

'Are you there?' asked Meredith looking towards the door to the bathroom.

She threw her feet out of bed and stepped on her pants sprawled on the floor. She put them on and looked a little further; her crop top and crazy-jean bum-short lay scattered near the entrance door. Now, Meredith was sure last night had happened and her memory wasn't illusory. She recalled she and the woman had arrived at her place about half an hour after midnight, and from the door, their hands were all over each other. The last thing Meredith remembered was the woman standing over her and decanting powder from a yellow capsule Meredith's mouth before shoving her naked onto the bed.

Meredith opened the door to the bathroom but no one was there. If she hadn't remembered the taste from kissing the woman's nicotine lips, or running her hands over her fully fleshed body, she would have thought she was delusional.

Meredith sat on her worn-out sofa and raked her hand through her hair in bewilderment, wondering why she could remember so very little from last night. How did she sleep so deeply not to know when the woman upped and left? Perhaps she was in a hurry and didn't want to disturb Meredith's sleep, or perhaps… Meredith found herself shuffling between questions, answers, and what was real and what wasn't.

Her phone rang. Meredith rushed to pick up.

'Hello.'

'Meredith!' Sarah, the voice on the other end of the phone yelled in a controlled tone. Meredith heaved a sigh and her shoulders fell. 'Where the fuck are you?'

'I am not feeling well,' Meredith answered.

'Really, Meredith!? Boss won't buy that shit, and neither will I.'

'Look, I'm in the middle of something. Will call you back.'

'Meredith, you better—'

Meredith ended the call in the middle of Sarah's sentence, just as the idea of going to the club to ask the barman if he knew… Meredith froze at that thought. The receipt! Her brain lit up. She rushed to her bum-short and pulled the paper receipt out with care. She scanned through, and at the top right corner of the receipt saw the name: Rachel Brown.

Meredith sat on the edge of her bed staring at the receipt contemplating her next action She reached for her phone, clicked on Google, cancelled, opened Instagram and type-searched Rachel Brown. Meredith searched through every profile with care. She opened the seventh profile and her eyes lit up with joy. It was the Rachel Brown she had met and made love to last night. Meredith followed her, and took her time through every post, liking each one and reading the captions beneath, then settled her gaze on a particular post after noticing it was the same house and the same blue car in the background of all the picture slides in the post. She zoomed in on the last slide and observed through the car window the sign of a Chinese restaurant opposite the house. Meredith checked the location at the top of the post; it read Bath Street. She went to Google and searched for Chinese restaurants in Bath Street, Scotland. The result; there was only one. She let out a wide smile. She had found the mystery woman.

In a few minutes, Meredith was in and out of the bathroom. She looked through her clothes rack in search of what to wear, something that would arouse in Rachel a longing to return to her bed. Meredith tried to imagine the excitement on Rachel Brown's face when she saw her, especially when she explained how she found her. Surely, Meredith thought, she would see through my determination and be impressed at my effort. Love is begun with time, she told herself, and time is effort.

Meredith remembered the green bubble-sleeve ruched floral bodycon dress she had purchased some months back. She had been surfing the internet when she stumbled upon the woven mini-dress, which featured an all-over floral shadow print and a plunging V-neckline, and thought to buy it for when an occasion arose to wear a fancy dress and not her usual ragged casualwear. She picked out the dress now as this was a fancy occasion.

When Meredith arrived at Bath Street, the first thing she did was look at the Chinese restaurant and whisper a thank-you. She then turned and focused her gaze on Rachel Brown's house, wondering what to do next; whether to knock on her door and say 'Surprise!', or just wait outside and hope she would come out anytime soon. Meredith spent the next five minutes contemplating her next line of action, and thought perhaps she had arrived too late and Rachel Brown had left home.

'That stupid driver,' she mouthed. Throughout the journey, she had felt he was driving too slowly and she had urged him to increase his speed. The first time she asked him to go faster, he looked back at her and said, 'Yeah, right,' in a disapproving manner, and for the rest of the journey, he just ignored her.

Meredith took a step forward, about to cross the road after deciding her best option would be to knock on Rachel Brown's door, but as her feet touched the ground, she placed her hand on her chest and began to inhale and exhale.

'Be calm, Meredith,' she said to herself, 'just be calm.'

The front door to the house opened, and Rachel Brown stepped out with a supermarket bag. She went to the boot of the blue car parked opposite the house – as it was in the picture – and placed the bag in it, then closed the car boot and was about to head back inside.

'Rachel Brown!' Meredith called and crossed to meet her.

Rachel swivelled and saw Meredith running towards her. Her eye popped wide. She opened her mouth but couldn't find the words to speak, and when Meredith embraced her, she broke free from the gesture.

'How the hell did you find me!?' Rachel asked bewildered.

'Are you not happy to see me?' asked Meredith, the excitement on her face disappearing.

'Happy! Are you—?' Rachel paused, looked to the front door of her house, then back to Meredith. 'I said how did you find me?' Rachel asked furiously.

'You forgot your receipt last night. It had your name on it,' Meredith replied with the receipt in her hand, while she stared at Rachel Brown with sadness, happy and confused all at the same time.

Rachel grabbed the receipt and looked through it. 'So you stalked me!? What are you? Twenty-two?'

'Twenty-two and a half. I am—' Meredith wanted to say but Rachel cut her short.

'I don't care,' yelled Rachel in a composed but furious voice. She looked at the front door of her house again then back to Rachel. 'Look, just get out of here. I never want to see you again or I will call the police on you.'

'Police!?' reiterated Meredith in dismay. 'I don't understand, what did I do?'

'Nothing, just—'

'What about last night?' Meredith continued, ignoring Rachel's attempt to interrupt. 'Didn't that mean anything to you? Did I not mean anything to you?'

'You're a big girl,' Rachel said trying not to be frustrated, 'stop acting like you lack love in your life, and get the fuck out of my mine.'

'I don't believe you,' said Meredith, attempting to touch Rachel, who rebuffed her. 'Do I not look good enough for you? If it's the sex I can be better, I've not had that much practice outside—

'I don't care,' Rachel shouted, 'just get out. My husband will be out soon!'

'Husband!' Meredith reiterated, addled. 'So last night was just fun for you?'

Rachel was about to reply when from behind her came a cheery masculine voice.

'Hey honey, you ready?'

'Yes honey,' Rachel feigned a sudden smile and threw her arm around the man. He was he husband. 'Just catching up with a friend,' she said pointing to Meredith.

Meredith looked defeated as she stared at the husband, who was handsome from the profundity of his eyes to the gentleness of his voice. The closer he got to her, the closer she felt to her world being crushed. And when he stretched his hand to her, she shook his warm hand which became cold and broke her heart all over again.

'A pleasure to meet you,' the man said. 'I haven't really met any of my wife's friends,' he said. 'I'm George, by the way.'

'I didn't know she had a husband too,' Meredith replied with a straight face and Rachel laughed out loud. George joined her.

'Well, now you know,' he said.

'Not to worry,' Rachel stepped in. 'Meredith isn't always around so you won't be seeing her.'

'In that case, Meredith, anytime you're around, please say hello.'

Meredith nodded.

'Honey, please wait for me in the car,' Rachel said to her husband, and waited until George was sitting in the driver's seat. She pulled Meredith aside. 'Forget about me, forget about last night, leave and never come back.'

Rachel let her go and flashed her a wide grin, then got into the car.

Meredith stood speechless watching Rachel and her husband drive away and wave to her. She tried to lift her hand to wave back, but she found that it was too heavy. A thousand thoughts and questions ran through her mind at the same time, and with each question she attempted to answer, she had a thousand and one more questions to ask.

Meredith looked up at the Chinese restaurant, slowly walked into it and sat by the window, staring at the front of the house where she had just been turned down.

'What would you like to have this morning?' a Chinese waitress asked Meredith in a polite tone ten minutes after she had sat numb. 'Ma'am,' the waitress leaned closer to Meredith. 'Can you hear me, ma'am?'

Meredith snapped out of her trance.

'Hi. Yes. Sorry, didn't hear what you said,' Meredith forced a smile but it was a failed attempt.

'I asked what you would like?'

'Oh, yeah. Anything.'

'Sorry, but could you be more specific? If you look through our menu, I believe you will find something you'll like.'

Meredith winced, picked up the menu and scanned through it.

'Tea,' she said. 'Just tea.'

'Okay.'

The waitress nodded and typed something into the device in her hand, bowed slightly at Meredith then started for the kitchen.

Meredith buried her head against the table in near tears as the feeling of foolishness and dejection flushed through her. The words Rachel Brown had said floated above and around her head without stay, and the more she thought about them, the more they sank deep into her.

For the eight years Meredith had spent in foster care, she had suffered from reactive attachment disorder, yet, four years after her care order had legally ended, her disorder had morphed into a collection of problematic symptoms which affected her mood, her anxiety levels, and her relationship with people. She saw the world through the eyes of the two sets of foster parents who had fostered her; evil and malicious, sexual predators and perverts. She hated every second of every minute of every day she spent in the foster system. It was not the system she had thought it was, or the system she was told it would be. She lived every day in pain, misery and hate, but above all, she lived in regret

Meredith's first foster parents, Mr and Mrs Benson, were everything evil. It didn't matter that she was young, and it was a middle-class evangelical Christian home, they physically abused and neglected her. Often times, she would go days without eating because her foster parents went on evangelism tours and left her alone without food or money. They derived joy from whipping her for any little thing, especially for things she had no idea about, and when items went missing in the house, she was always the culprit, it didn't matter if she was guilty or not. At night, they locked the kitchen door so she could not drink water, and she became used to drinking water from the toilet. At first, when her social worker visited, she made attempts to report the conditions she was living in but failed in every attempt because Mr and Mrs Benson made a good show of a happy family during home visits. The only time she almost succeeded, the social worker laughed it off, and later that night, Meredith received the beating of her life. Soon enough, her social worker no longer visited, and she spent the next three years of her life living in hell. Meredith only left that home after Mr Benson died and his wife accused her of being the witch who had caused his cancer. She sent Meredith back to the group home.

When Meredith moved into her second foster home at the ripe age of fifteen, she was glad her new foster parents; Mr and Mrs Duncan, didn't act maliciously towards her. Two weeks after she moved in, Mr Duncan ordered her to make his bed in his bedroom. As she went about it, he entered the room almost behind her, locked the bedroom door and forced himself on her. Meredith cried. That night, when she was home alone with Mrs Duncan, she garnered courage and reported the sexual assault on her. Mrs Duncan took Meredith into the bedroom, and told her to do on her everything she had done to her husband. Meredith never had a normal life after her experience; her idea of love and sex became totally skewed. It got worse, especially when they began to sleep with her together. Meredith endured till she was sixteen and filed for her care order to stop. The court process ended as soon as it began because Mr and Mrs Duncan listed her disorders as the reason why she was too immature to become independent and experience the real world. When they got home after the judgement, Mr Duncan whipped her for her attempt to be independent, which would have meant they would stop receiving her foster care money and other grants for expenses as a result of her disorders. She endured another two years of abuse until her foster care order legally ended.

Meredith existed in two foster homes in her eight years of being in the system, but her experiences made it seem like she was born in the system. She was nothing but a form of passive income for her foster parents. She struggled with her emotions. She eventually got to learn the meaning of love, but it still didn't resonate with her as she saw herself as too damaged to love or be loved. Her lack of empathy was obvious at the inception of her independence, but she managed to conceal it behind her lowness; her post-traumatic stress disorder, however, came often and without warning.

Rachel Brown came into Meredith's life at the time Meredith was struggling with the freedom that came with independence, and at the same time, struggling to break free from her past and her pain. It was why at first blush with Rachel Brown, she was goggle-eyed. She had felt a certain kind of comfort around her, a feeling of peace and a non-judgemental voice towards her past and present. She had felt, finally, that she could be who she wanted to become.

The more Meredith thought about it, the more hurt she felt; naked, vulnerable and broken, as the trauma of instability drowned her again. In one brief night of the many nights she had lived, she had found a sense of identity only to wake and lose it again. Every ounce of pain she had felt through her years in the foster homes, her mother's unwillingness to fight to have her back home, and her inability to resist her abusers, coursed through her veins. She formed a fist and cast a frown. She wasn't going to allow herself to be used again.

Meredith heard a teacup land on the table. She lifted her head and her eyes were red.

'Here is your tea,' said the Chinese waitress.

Meredith looked up, and the waitress was flashing her a smile. 'Wait,' said Meredith wrapping her palm around the cup. It was warm, and it reminded her of the warmth of George's hand.

'How can I be of further assistance?' the waitress asked.

Meredith stared out of the window as the blue car drove back up the driveway. George stepped out of it and into his house. Rachel Brown wasn't with him.

'What does it feel like being used?' she turned to the waitress.

After a few seconds of silence, the Chinese waitress flashed a grin, but Meredith knew it was insincere, as it was required of people in the business of hospitality to always smile.

'I won't know how to answer that, as the word used is subjective. How we react depends on the situation and circumstances.'

Meredith looked into the tea in her hand with ambivalence, and as if inspired by the tea asked almost at once. 'Have you ever been used?'

'We all have,' replied the Chinese waitress, and Meredith thought she was being diplomatic with her response. 'But nobody likes to be used,' the waitress added.

For the first time, Meredith flashed the waitress a wide grin, which grew into a malicious one. She set down the tea, took out money from her purse and handed it to the waitress. 'Thank you for the conversation,' she said and walked away. The waitress looked at the cup; the tea was untouched.

Meredith walked across the road to Rachel's house with slow steps and a renewed vigour, walking against the wind. She stopped by the car, stared at it like it was a strange object, winced, and started for the front door of the house. She knocked. She was about to knock again a few seconds later when the door opened. It was George Brown.

'Hey,' George smiled. 'Meredith, right?'

'Very right,' Meredith said. 'I didn't think you would remember.'

'I try not to forget a name,' George said, then leaned forward and whispered, 'but that is only because I tend to forget.'

They both laughed.

'I was on my way back when I saw your car. Thought it would be nice to see your wife before I leave.'

'Oh, yeah. That would have been nice, but she isn't home.'

'Ouch,' Meredith exclaimed. 'And I really wanted to see her. It's been a long time since we had a chat.' She heaved a sigh. 'I guess some other time then.'

'Wait,' George called as Meredith turned to leave. 'You could stay and wait, she won't be long gone. I dropped her at the supermarket just by the corner.'

'Yeah?'

'Yeah. She will be back anytime now. Come in and wait.'

'Okay, thanks,' Meredith said and walked in.

'Please give me a minute, I was in the kitchen before you knocked.'

'It's fine, take your time.'

'What should I get you?'

'Anything strong will do.'

'All right. Make yourself at home.'

George went into the kitchen.

Meredith sat, and almost drowned in the comfortable navy velvet three-seater sofa in the sitting room. She shifted her gaze across to the dining room and her eyes caught the array of kitchen cutlery held in a transparent box atop the grey Brittany dining table in the middle of the room. She wondered why they had a six- set table when only two people lived in the house. Perhaps they have kids, Meredith thought, but she looked up at the picture frames hanging on the wall, and there were no children in them. The more she stared at the pictures, the more she wondered why Rachel Brown had made out with her, if her husband knew she was bi, or if she did it to punish him and it was her first time, but then she remembered the sex, and knew it was no first timer's feeling.

'Sorry to keep you waiting,' said George from behind Meredith.

Meredith turned to him with a smile, and he handed her a drink.

'Gin and soda cocktail,' George told her.

'Thank you. Nice place you've got here.'

'Well,' said George with false humility, 'what can I say?'

Meredith rose and started towards the wall of pictures. She took down a medium-sized framed photograph of George and Rachel Brown cuddling in laughter, just above where the television sat. She stared at Rachel with admiration and rubbed Rachel's cheeks, which made George cringe.

He cleared his throat.

'So how long have you known my wife?' asked George.

Meredith snapped back to life and returned the picture to the wall.

'A couple of years,' Meredith replied, but from the way George looked at her, she felt the need to say more to convince him. 'We went to the same high school.'

'You lived in Mexico?' George asked with enthusiasm.

'No,' Meredith replied with a disdainful gesture.

'Then how did you attend the same high school? My wife's high school was in Mexico.'

Meredith swallowed.

'That was a joke,' Meredith broke into a laugh. 'I lived in Mexico for a short while because my father was in the military and moved every now and then. My time in Mexico was unpleasant, and your wife was the only good thing that happened to me,' she added.

'Yeah, I know,' replied George. 'She is the best thing that has happened to me too.'

'I can imagine,' Meredith joked, but beneath her breath she cursed him. 'How long have you been married for?'

'Three years and counting,' George answered with a wide grin and flashed Meredith his ring.

'The ring suits your skin,' Meredith said, masking her irritation behind a smile. 'She is so thoughtful.'

'I know, right,' George said with a smug grin. 'She really is.'

Meredith turned to the dining table, staring at the Brittany, then pointed to a painting on the wall.

'I love that,' she said and started towards the painting.

'That is a breath-taking moment which shows men of the Igbo culture of Nigeria dancing in their native way. It's quite an interesting piece by Lujys, a Nigerian artist.'

Meredith furrowed her brow and sipped from her drink.

'Tell me more about you and my wife. Barely ever met any of her friends.'

'What would you like to know?' asked Meredith, then cast a quick glance at the cutlery on the Brittany, which included two medium kitchen knives.

'Everything possible,' replied George.

'Where do I begin?' Meredith heaved a sigh as her mind toggled between last night at the club and her bedroom. 'I don't know whether our meeting was fate or chance, but whichever it was, I loved it, still do. Our meeting was electric; it was like we'd known each other for years. She knew every part of me that I didn't know existed, and I didn't want it to end.'

'Are we still talking about my wife?' George asked, staring at her, confused.

Meredith snapped out of her reminiscing, and stared at George with a blank gaze. There was a knock on the door. George kept his gaze on Meredith and after a few seconds flashed a grin and said, 'That should be my wife,' he went to the door.

Meredith rushed to the Brittany, grabbed a kitchen knife and hid it behind her as she heard Rachel's voice crowding her husband's, and approaching the sitting room.

'Hello, Rachel Brown,' said Meredith to Rachel.

Rachel froze and the bags in her hand fell to the floor.

'It's what I was trying to tell you,' George whispered to Rachel.

'Can I have a word with you?' Rachel said to her husband. 'In the kitchen, now,' she added as she started for the kitchen without acknowledging Meredith.

The glee on Meredith's face disappeared, and slowly turned dour. She fixed her gaze on the entrance of the kitchen, devoid of hope, and consumed by a growing rage in her head.

When Rachel and her husband stepped out of the kitchen and back into the sitting room, George called her name, but Meredith didn't hear.

'Meredith,' George called again, a little more aggressively than the first time, and Meredith snapped out of her thoughts.

'I think it is time you left.'

Meredith shifted her gaze to Rachel Brown, who was staring back at her, grim, but Rachel didn't flinch. She emptied her drink, placed the glass on the table and took baby step towards the door, but stopped in front of Rachel.

'Rachel Brown, I love you.'

'What!?' George frowned. 'My wife was right, you're crazy. Get out of my house and never come back,' he said, then grabbed her by the shoulder, intending to drag her out.

Meredith plunged the knife into his stomach, twisting it with a swift motion. Rachel lunged forward to wrestle the knife away, but Meredith was quicker, yanking the knife and holding it to his neck, the blade biting deep. Blood sprayed outward, spattering everywhere.

'Come any closer and I will drive this knife through his neck.'

Rachel froze, her eyes locked on the knife in Meredith's hand. She considered making a grab for it, but something in Meredith's expression stopped her. Instead, she slowly lifted her hands in surrender. 'Whatever it is you want you can have it. Money, jewelry, whatever. I won't even call the police, just please let him go.'

'You think this is about the money!?' Meredith frowned. 'No, Rachel, I'm doing this because I love you.'

"Meredith, you don't know what you're saying...". Rachel was cut short by George's attempt to grab the knife. Meredith jabbed him in the stomach with the butt of the knife, hitting exactly where she'd stabbed.

'Stay where you are!' she warned as Rachel made an attempt to help her husband.

Rachel stood still, helpless, watching her husband writhe in pain.

'Grab that tape and bind your wife,' Meredith ordered gesturing to the duct tape on the table.

'Go to hell.'

'I could send you there faster if you continue this way.' She held the knife to his, and after a few tense moments of silence, George gave a slight nod. She guided him to the table and did as was told, binding Rachel's hands with the tape, careful not to bind it too tight. Despite the faint numbness creeping up his spine from the blood loss, his gaze fell on a glint of metal peeking out from beneath the table cloth. A pocket knife, forgotten in the chaos lay inches away from him.

'My husband is bleeding,' Rachel said to Meredith in a tender voice.

Meredith turned George over. His hand was placed over his stomach, all covered in red. Not wanting him to bleed to death before the show began, she tore a piece of his shirt and handed it back to him. George stumbled to a corner, folding the piece of cloth over his wound.

'If you love me as you say," Rachel continued, "let me take him to the hospital'.

Meredith winced. 'Don't push your luck.'

'I know why you are here,' George said weakly, his blood turning his grey shirt red. 'Why?'

Meredith replied.

'You want to feel loved. You want to love.'

Meredith, taking a seat wondered what foolishness he was about to spew, 'What makes you think that?'

'Only someone desperate for love would go to the lengths that you're going. I can help you. We can help you.'

'No honey,' Rachel cut in. 'What she needs is the psychiatric hospital, and not our help. She is mentally sick.'

'You're both right,' said Meredith, wanting to believe the hope she thought she heard in George's voice, 'but I am far from being helped. Even Broadmoor can't help me if they wanted to.'

'Oh please,' Rachel scoffed, 'you're a manipulative bastard who wants us to feel pity for you, but I see right through it, through you. you're mentally deranged, and you belong behind bars.'

Meredith chuckled.

'What is funny?' asked Rachel.

'That you believe in a failed system. The government, the police, healthcare, tax. They are all a sham, it's how they control us, mould us into how they want us to be. And until you realize real help comes from within, and that the system is the last place to turn to for help, you'd remain lost.'

'How perfect!' Rachel exclaimed. 'Just another one of you blaming the government for your warp mind.'

'You are right,' Meredith let out a sad sigh. 'I can't totally blame them, as much as I want to. Part of the reason I turned out this way is because of me.'

George and Rachel exchanged confused glances, then George shifted his gaze back to Meredith, then settled his eyes on the knife in her hand.

'They say we can identify as who, or what we like.' Meredith scoffed reflectively, 'Even as kids, we were told that. Can you imagine!?' Meredith scowled. 'One day, my teacher taught us about trees. I told my mum I wanted to identify as a tree and she rebuked me. Stupid me didn't let it end there, my teacher and principal held a meeting with my mum and she told them to their face that as long as I was her child, I will identify as a girl. Social workers got involved, said my mum was unfit to be my mum.' She paused and mulled over the statement then turned to George, 'does that make any sense!?' George shook his head. 'I was ten when they took me and promised a safe space, a safe home.'

Meredith turned to George and noticed the piece of cloth over his stomach was soaked. She looked about and found two napkins on the dining table, grabbed and handed it to George.

'Thank you,' George said, his voice oozing of ambivalence.

'For the longest time,' Meredith continued, 'I blamed my mum. If only she had fought hard enough to not let me go.'

'It wouldn't have made any difference,' George said to Meredith.

'She could have tried,' Meredith replied looking dejected. 'From that age till I was eighteen, I was physically and sexually abused. I was depressed for as long as I can remember. Until I met you, Rachel Brown.'

'Do I look like a fool?' Rachel mocked. 'Just one night and suddenly I am your ray of hope!? You're delusional.'

'Wait!' George said, trying to sit upright. He applied a bit more pressure to the wound, waited till his breath was calm and shifted his gaze between his wife and Meredith. 'What do you mean, one night?'

Meredith looked to Rachel as if to ask 'Are you going to tell him or should I?'

Rachel swallowed. This isn't how she hoped to tell George. In fact, if she had her way, he probably would never have found out. She opened her mouth to speak, but the right words wouldn't come out.

'Your wife is a lesbian. We fucked,' Meredith broke in.

Rachel closed her eyes in despair as George looked at her, confusion etched all-over his paling face.

'I don't understand what she's saying' he said, still looking at Rachel, waiting for her to say something. Her silence was all the confirmation he needed.

'I can explain,' Rachel said, tears dripping down her cheeks.

'Can you now?' George asked, slowly letting his hand loosen the pressure on his stomach.

'I know that tone,' Rachel said, "you're disappointed in me."

'Disappointed!?' he shook his head. 'I am dying.'

Rachel's tears flowed freely and George was getting increasingly more lightheaded, from the blood loss and now this revelation.

'I am sure you must have also figured out that we are not friends,' Meredith said to George, 'We met last night and had amazing sex. It was the best night of my life.'

'Can you shut up?!' George ordered, he didn't need her butting into what could very well be his last conversation with his wife.

'Was she your first?' George asked. Rachel shook her head and George closed his eyes as a sharp pain jolted through his chest. He leaned his head back and tears rolled down his cheeks, his head still finding difficulty comprehending all that was happening. 'When did this begin?'

'About a year ago. Maybe more.'

George stared at her, distraught.

'Anytime I was pissed off at you, I'd go out to find a girl I could make out with. I love women too,' Rachel whispered.

'But you never told me you did.'

'I am sorry," Rachel cried, "but it doesn't change the fact that I love you. Always did and always will.'

George attempted to make a mockery laughter, but instead, he coughed up blood. He looked at his stomach and grunted lightly. 'I think it's infected. I'm beginning to feel warm inside.'

'No, please,' Rachel said, making an attempt to stand, but Meredith pointed the knife at her, then to George.

'Can I ask you a question?' George said to Rachel, 'And be honest, I am dying anyways. Is this why you don't want to have a child with me?'

Rachel closed her eyes, exhaled and nodded.

'And I always thought it was because you saw me as unfit and slothful'

'No, George,' Rachel replied, 'far from it. Everything about you is perfect. You are not the problem, I am.'

George flashed her a stupefied gaze.

Meredith poked leaned her head backwards, staring at the two lovers enthralled.

'I was also worried that if I got pregnant, you would no longer find me attractive. I'd add some extra kilos and lose shape, get morning sickness, a faster heartbeat, post-partum depression, protruding belly. I just couldn't deal with that.'

'Have I ever made you feel that way? Now you're just making excuses because you and I know I would never have treated you like that.'

'How could I have known? People change' Rachel retorted, even though she knew she was wrong.

'At least I would have been able to kiss your protruding belly every day when I woke, and before I slept,' George chuckled in pain. Rachel chuckled too.

'That would have been nice to see.'

'Yeah,' George nodded. He leaned his head back against the wall, mulled for a few seconds, and exhaled. 'You always said one of the reasons you love me is because I was understanding.'

Rachel nodded.

'Why didn't you tell me? We could have talked about it. Maybe even agreed to wait till you were ready.'

'Would you have waited?'

George heaved a sigh and looked at his bleeding stomach. 'I guess now we will never know.'

'I am sorry,' Rachel cried.

'I know,' replied George, his eyes shifting to the pocket knife on the table. He managed to rise, and he started towards Rachel.

'What do you think you're doing? Meredith asked him, bemused.

'What does it look like,' George replied without stopping. 'Going to make up with my wife.'

'After all you just heard?' Meredith countered. 'She has been cheating on you with random women! Women not men! That should hurt you even more.'

'It does, but I'm dying' George replied.

'So what about her cheating? Betrayal? Disrespect...'

'I am hurt Meredith," George said in his most calming voice, 'but I'm dying and, I don't want to spend my last moments being angry at someone who I love this much. Life is short, simple, yet profound, and I will not hold back from appreciating what life has given me. You shouldn't either. You should smell the roses while you still can.

He knelt before Rachel and embraced her. Meredith began to sob.

George shot Meredith a sidelong glance and swiftly grabbed the pocket knife. He placed it in Rachel's hands and whispered, 'I love you.'

Rachel felt the knife in her palms and began to shake her head. George held her still, caressed her cheeks, and they touched foreheads. 'I'm sorry,' he said.

Meredith wiped her tears and stood to separate the couple. 'That's enough. I didn't come here to see you two make up.' She grabbed George and shoved him back into the corner where he had sat. George fell on his stomach and screamed aloud.

Rachel cried and looked up at Meredith. 'Please, help him, he is dying.' Meredith flashed Rachel a detached glance, causing her to flinch. 'Your plan is for him to die.'

Meredith smirked and bowed her head slightly.

George moaned and sat upright, coughing up blood. He looked down at his stomach, the napkin was soaked. He threw it away and heaved a sigh. 'No need for that,' he said to Meredith. 'I've already lost enough blood.' He shifted his gaze to his wife, who was really sobbing. He cast a long, grief-stricken glance at her then made a slight nod.

Rachel closed her eyes and nodded too. When she opened her eyes, they were full with cruelty. She gripped the pocket knife tight and sliced through the tape that bound her.

'You want to know something,' Rachel said to Meredith.

'What?'

'Last night was the worst night I've ever spent with a woman. I approached you because I could smell your vulnerability from where I stood. I hoped I could create a lasting connection with you, and make you the only woman I fuck, but no, I hated every moment with you. It's why I left without saying a word.'

'That's a lie,' Meredith said, shaking her head. 'You're saying that to make me feel bad, and I won't fall for it.'

'You're miserable, and you blame everybody except yourself for it,' Rachel continued in an abrasive tone.

'I blame myself too.'

'No. You just say that to yourself to feel good.'

Meredith covered her head with her hands as if to prevent it from exploding. 'No. Stop it,' she cried, 'you are messing with my head.'

'Your father probably abandoned you...

'Shut up!'

'Your mother didn't fight for you,' Rachel continued with an upsurge in her voice.

'Shut up!' Meredith warned, pacing and blocking her ears.

'The foster parents who were supposed to take care of you showed you no love. Did you ever ask yourself why? It is because you are not lovable.'

'Get out of my head,' Meredith pointed the knife at her.

'If you thought coming here and killing my husband would in some way force me to love you, you thought wrong, because I would rather die than love a person like you.'

Meredith charged towards Rachel with the knife, but George garnered strength and grabbed Meredith by the foot, tripping her, the knife slipping from her hands.

Rachel, desperately tried to cut through the tape binding her hands.

George, with whatever little strength he had left, wrestled with Meredith, trying to stop her from retrieving the knife. In one swift moment, she jabbed his bleeding wound, grabbed the knife and drove it into his chest just as the bind around Rachel's hand broke free.

Meredith covered her mouth with her hands as she watched George stagger back, his bloody hands struggling to grab the knife's handle, but he fell to the ground, dead.

Almost trembling, Meredith swivelled to Rachel, and just as she was about to open her mouth to speak, Rachel charged towards her with the pocket knife. Meredith attempted to pull the knife from George's chest, but Rachel reached her first, and in three quick successions, drove the pocket knife into her stomach.

Meredith stared at Rachel, startled, as she staggered back. Her blood spattering. She fell on her stomach, and began to crawl towards the door.

Rachel cried over her husband's body, attempting to hold his face, but her hands were shaking. She kissed her hand and placed it on his forehead. 'Till we meet again,' she whispered and closed his eyes.

Her countenance changed, she turned to face Meredith.

'Where do you think you're going?' Rachel said, watching as Meredith writhed to grab the door knob but couldn't turn it. 'You made a mistake finding me,' she said as she strode towards Meredith. 'You made a mistake coming here. And you made the biggest mistake, killing my husband.'

Rachel stood over Meredith and turned her onto her back. She crouched and placed the pocket knife on Meredith's throat.

'Can I ask you a favour?' Meredith said, 'Before you kill me, even if it's a lie, tell me you love me,' she said, trying to touch Rachel on the cheek.

Rachel, with cold eyes, and calm fingers, slit through Meredith's throat from one side to the other. She watched the life go out of Meredith's eyes, and said with a cold, gleaming gaze, she said, 'I hate you.'

FAKE LONDON GIRL

It takes strong will – stronger will I should say – to come out of a habit; a bad habit most especially. I have been there, and so have you. We have all been here. We've lived a fake life laden with lies, pretence and worse; the aftermath of evil which tends to come with living a lie. It all begins with a lie, one simple innocent lie, but to cover that lie, we tell a million more lies and then the lying never ends. It takes a simple heart, a telltale heart, and above all a spirit-filled heart to live a lie and be stupidly brave to confess and relive the truth. Not many can boast of such stupidity. But she, Priscilla Igwe, the story of whom I am about to tell, with injudicious bravado took an unusual turn and that made all the difference.

'Chai, our daughter is home!' exclaimed an older man. His eyes were wide open, as was his mouth too, eager to continue talking. 'When I heard you have come, I was so glad,' he turned to the crowd behind him. They cheered and urged him on.; he let out a smug grin and continued to speak. 'And when they told me you had come all the way from *obodo oyibo*, I knew I must come to touch you so that I too can boast before I die that I touched an *oyibo*,' he giggled and the others burst into loud cheers and laughter. When they had quietened down, Mama led them to where the others were already sitting, drinking and eating in celebration of the arrival of Priscilla Igwe, many of whom she barely knew or didn't know at all.

'I will join you people soon,' Priscilla motioned and started for the opposite end of the compound, shifting her gaze and welcoming the throng that trooped in. *Are people in this town so jobless?* she wondered beneath her feigned smile. She was done for, all because of a statement, a metonymy which was supposed to have passed for humour. She had been away too long to remember that Anagara people had no sense of humour.

She bit her lips and flung her head down; she had found a corner to lie low in, away from the increasing crowd who were beginning to cheer in drunken jubilation. It was obvious they were being inspired by the bottles of beer spread across the tables before them. She needed her own form of inspiration. Letting out a heavy sigh, she closed her eyes and remembered a billboard sign which she had one time come across in Lagos. It read: *When bewildered, close your eyes and listen to your inner voice, let it inspire, let it guide you.* She obeyed. Sixty seconds after and she heard no voice. She opened her eyes cursing that moment when it all began, when she lied – no, it wasn't a lie, it was a figurative way of referring to the city of Lagos, a simple comparison of how Lagos is to Nigeria as London is to the United Kingdom but smaller.

'So if grandma illness had not gotten worse, you wouldn't have come home?' Priscilla's cousin had asked with a frown when Priscilla first arrived.

'No, I still would have come home. I was already planning on returning when I heard about the state of her health.'

'I see,' she whispered. 'So where have you been all these years? Nobody knew your whereabouts; you just snuck out of Anagara as if you had stolen maize from the village storehouse, or did you?'

Priscilla chuckled and so did some family members and neighbours who had come to welcome her.

'I have been hustling in small London,' replied Priscilla with a smile.

'*Chai*! London!' exclaimed someone in a loud voice who started running out of the compound shouting: 'Priscilla *bia si* London ooo! *Priscilla bia si London.*'

His words led to an outburst of cheering. Her mother, Mama, as she was popularly called, motioned to Priscilla to go in to change her clothes then return to do as custom demanded – to wet the elders' mouths with food and drink to mark her safe journey back home after long years of being away. She had no idea that she was going to be feeding the town.

She lifted her gaze towards the jubilant crowd then to the compound entrance. Their neighbour, Tobe, was walking into the compound with less enthusiasm, and was obviously, from her manufactured smile, trying hard to hide an agony. Tobe went to meet Mama and whispered something in her ear, and in an instant both their faces turned grim. The way Mama took Tobe aside to whisper something to her intensified that feeling. Tobe nodded and started away.

'Tobe my baby,' Priscilla called out. 'Why haven't you come to celebrate my return? *Haba*! Is that how life is?'

Tobe stood quiet, as if pondering what to say. She opened her mouth to speak but froze, closed and opened her eyes, and after a loud pained sigh, she said, 'My father is dead.'

Priscilla said nothing, somewhat dumb and consumed by guilt at having misjudged the poor girl.

'I am sorry, I didn't know.'

'Your mother said you will both come visiting later, when your guests have gone.'

'They are not my guests,' Priscilla wanted to say, but bit back her words and instead said 'I will go with you now. Mama can handle the guests in my absence.'

They walked in silence. Tobe ushered Priscilla into the less busy compound filled with goats and chickens with red ropes tied around their neck and ankle, as they run and excrete around the compound. Priscilla thought they were no different from the men and women drinking in hers.

'Nothing has changed,' said Priscilla. 'Anagara is just as I remember it.'

Tobe flashed a grin and pulled aside the yellow wrapper which was the door into the house. They bowed their heads and went in.

There was loud wailing and mourning, the loudest coming from Tobe's mother, who was being consoled at the end of the room. Priscilla began greeting as she made her way to her. The mourners on looking up to return the greeting budged the person sitting next to them to make them look up to see who it was offering the greetings. Soon, the mourning turned into incessant stares and pleasing whispers. Priscilla tried to imagine what they were whispering about, then resolved not to, as the smiles plastered across their faces told it all.

'I see your *chi* has not left you even though you left us,' said Tobe's mother to Priscilla with a snivelling voice.

Priscilla grinned. 'It is not like that, ma. I was only…'

'In small London!?' Tobe's mother cut in, wobbling her head. 'We heard. But what is small in London? My daughter, London is London.'

'It is her humility that made her call it small,' one of the mourners said aloud and the others nodded in agreement.

Priscilla feigned a grin, unsure how to contradict the claim of having lived in London.

'Welcome home,' Tobe's mother continued. 'It is of course no coincidence your returning home and the death of my husband. That your *chi* brought you back home at this difficult time has a meaning.' The women surrounding her exclaimed, nodding their heads. 'It is obvious you will be a pillar in his death.'

'God be blessed,' a mourner said in low voice.

'You know you were his favourite neighbour,' Tobe's mother said to Priscilla then paused, and began to cry, using the back of her hand to prevent her tears from flowing down further.

'Don't cry,' Priscilla cuddled her, 'please don't cry, or at least try not to. You'll only end up sick and not bring back your husband.' She heaved a sigh. 'I can't imagine the kind of pain you're going through, but I want to help.'

'Help her carry her pain?' asked a woman, bewildered.

'Maybe that is how they do it in London,' replied another woman in a low monotone.

'Not at all,' Priscilla replied to both women, then returned her face to Anagara's newest widow. 'I will help by giving you and your family two hundred and fifty thousand naira, for the burial.'

Priscilla's words evoked a sudden kind of silence in the room. Everyone froze, as did their tears.

Mama Tobe broke the shocked silence with a song of praise.

* * * *

Grandma opened her mouth as if to say something, but only air passed through before she shut it again. Her near lifeless body was an unbearable sight to behold. Grandma's room was the only place Priscila found she could hide away and not be disturbed, but not long after she settled in Mama came to tell her some titled chiefs had just arrived in their compound and had come to greet and wish Grandma well.

'That is a lie,' Priscilla protested. 'They came to eat from the bag of money I brought from London.'

It has been a month since her return home and people had not stopped visiting. It looked to her like her family had forgotten they were all gathered here because Grandma, in what seem to be her last moments on earth, had asked everyone to return home, and not because she had returned with a bag of money she earned from living in *small London*.

'The first goat we bought wasn't big enough.' Mama said, ignoring her protest, then added 'Give Oluchi money to buy a bigger one for your well-wishers,' as she walked away.

'Well-wishers my foot,' Priscilla retorted with a resigned look. She swivelled to the wooden window fit with red-brick walls, then settled her gaze on Grandma, exhaling. She needed someone to talk to, someone to share her fears and joy with. She no longer trusted her friend, Juliet, enough to share her deepest worries with her. How could she tell Juliet she had been living a lie since her arrival? That the British accent she had been practising and now carefully spoke was fake? The whole of Anagara would in no time learn of her secret and mock her till something or someone else had better reason to be mocked. She reminded herself of when they were teenagers and she had confided in Juliet about her one night stand with a chief's son. Two days after, it became the gossip in the market square while villagers traded. On confronting Juliet, she learnt her friend had told several people but made them promise to keep it a secret.

The silence in the room inflamed her thought and echoed her worries. She looked out of the window to the people eating and enjoying themselves, and for the first time, she understood what it meant to be surrounded by people yet be lonely. There is a harsh kind of pain when one is physically lonely, but when one is mentally alone, unable to share one's thoughts and feelings – be it joy or sadness – with someone else, that in itself is the worst kind of pain, a sting of death which slowly ruptures the mind.

Within her one month of returning back home, Priscilla had attained an informal *Ndi Nze* status as a result of her living in *small London*, and helping almost half of the town with financial favours. Her new status meant she was restricted and could no longer do the little simple things she loved like taking a stroll in the gentleness of the night, plucking *agbalumo* from the gigantic African cherry tree by the riverside, cracking jokes to and about random strangers at the town square. However much she missed those little things, she couldn't deny loving the prestige that came with being highly honoured amongst men and women, some older than her. It was only last Saturday when elders were debating over an issue during the monthly town hall meeting; she arrived thirty minutes late, yet her entrance was met with a hall of silence and cheerful whispers, everyone motioning her towards them to sit but she kept rebuffing them with a smile till she sat at the edge of the last seat in the hall. For her sake, the moderator recapped all the ideas that had been brought forward on how to tackle the town's poor crop cultivation, and how every one of those ideas depended on financial strength which the town lacked, then ended by asking her what she thought about the ideas.

'They are all good ideas,' she answered. 'And agriculture as we know it is a vital trade in our town. I will contribute towards this development by donating a hundred and fifty thousand naira.' At the end of her words came a loud cheer, and the repeated singing of her name which brought an end to the meeting an hour earlier than proposed.

'Aunty Priscilla,' called Oluchi as she ran into the room. They were cousins, but she referred to Priscilla as aunty due to the difference in their age. 'The butcher has brought the goat and Mama said I should collect the money from you.'

Priscilla exhaled, reached into her purse and handed Oluchi some hard currencies. Oluchi counted and lifted a five-hundred-naira note.

'This is extra. Should I take it?'

'Yes.'

'Yeeeeeeee!' Oluchi shouted as she twirled. 'Thank you, ma,' she said and started to hurry away but stopped by the door.

'Aunty, will you tell us stories about London tonight?'

With a wide grin, Priscilla replied. 'Yes I will.'

Oluchi dashed off yelling and throwing her hands in the air. Priscilla watched her through the window telling the other kids and how they threw their hands in the air. She wondered why the excitement, especially knowing that they barely understood the stories which she told in a British accent, but they laughed anyway, probably at her poor imitation of the accent.

As she wallowed in the euphoria of the moments birthed by her lie, it became apparent by the day that she was running out of money in her bag to fund her new lifestyle. She left the window view and went to sit beside Grandma, stroking her forehead. Grandma was her best friend; they spoke about anything and everything. She remembered having narrated to her the awkward taste of her first kiss to which Grandma laughed and reassured her it would taste and feel better at her next attempt. Her husband was no different from her, but he now lived in memory. His death was chary, no one dared talk about it for fear of being a victim too. That was probably the only thing she and Grandma never spoke about, not even when her son, Priscilla's father, died in the same manner.

'What are you doing here?' came a voice from behind. Priscilla swivelled to see Juliet strolling in.

'Don't you know those men downstairs are here to see you?' Juliet said.

'They want to see *omo* London and she is not in the mood to see any of them.'

Juliet nodded her head, amused, turned to Grandma and greeted her.

'All you people that have money, ehn! You will just be jumping from one mood to another. Since when is there a special mood for receiving visitors again?'

Priscilla grinned in a mocking gesture then thought Grandma did the same too.

'How have you been?'

'How else can I be when I have been living in Anagara since the day my mother poured me out? I would definitely feel better in a place like London. Look at your skin!'

Priscilla chuckled.

'That London must be a gold mine,' Juliet continued. '*Shebi* you will take me along when you're returning?'

'It is not as simple as that. It requires a lot of paper work.'

'Is it not paper? Don't worry, we will cross the bridge when we get there. I will *sha* fly inside plane *abi*?'

'Yes,' Priscilla replied laughing.

Juliet flew her hand into the air through the window, then leaned on the windowsill staring into the air daydreaming.

'I am surprised you're not with the people drinking and eating?' asked Priscilla.

'I was going to ask you the same thing,' retorted Juliet. 'What are you doing here alone?'

'I am not alone,' replied Priscilla shifting her gaze to Grandma.

Juliet swivelled to Grandma and shook her head. 'You are.'

Priscilla grinned.

'The men coming around, have you found any of them interesting enough for a fling or marriage?'

Priscilla shook her head.

'And has any approached you?'

Priscilla shook her head again. Juliet looked out the window in awe.

'Really!? You mean to tell me none of these men has shown interest in you?'

'None that I know of,' Priscilla shook her head, trying hard to conceal her disappointed gaze.

'Hmm!' Juliet mulled for a few seconds. 'Well I understand. A fine rich girl like you will have plenty rich men lined up behind her, why would you want to settle for an Anagara man?' she chuckled. 'I won't be surprised if the next time you visit home you bring along a white husband.'

Priscilla opened her mouth to say something but shut it at once. She didn't see the need in telling her friend that she had no man in her life, and those she had back in Lagos only came and went for fun.

'You wouldn't understand my plight,' was all Priscilla said.

'Try me.'

'I have a problem,' said Priscilla and Juliet laughed out loud.

'You rich people are always funny,' she said, shifting her gaze to Grandma. Grandma's eye prickled at her and her laughter dried out. She swivelled back to Priscilla.

'You have a problem!?' she reiterated. 'Look my friend, money solves all problems. Let your money solve yours,' she said letting out an unassuming giggle then looked at Grandma's eyes --she was asleep.

* * * *

At night, Priscilla sat not too far from the bonfire, within close range of where every member of her family sat. She gazed from one end of the compound to the other, amazed at how people gathered to honour Grandma by singing sweet songs and telltales of her youthful days.

'I am proud of you, Grandma.'

'*O eziokwu, kwenyere,*' a handsome young man in full Igbo regalia replied her.

Priscilla swivelled towards him, realising she had spoken out loud. She understood his Ibo to mean he agreed with her, but it was impossible to reply in Ibo using a British accent.

'Thank you,' she replied.

'*I na- acho na i na site n'ebe di anya ele gi anya,*' he laughed, finding his words funny. '*Inime oku enwere ihe ka ahu e nwere?*'

Priscilla laughed quietly, feigning ignorance. 'I really do not understand what you said but I am flattered regardless.'

'Unfortunately, my English is not as pure as yours,' the man told her in broken English, 'and I can barely hear what you say with the accent you speak in.'

She chortled in a polite manner and called on Oluchi. 'Oluchi, can you please help interpret what he says in Igbo, and to him what I say in English?'

'Of course, aunty, *Nwa nne nwanyi!*' she exclaimed. 'What else am I here for? Let him shoot his shot, *nkwanu*,' she said sizing the man from head to toe, then scoffed.

'That is what staying in London for too long can cause,' joked Priscilla and Oluchi laughed. Oluchi turned to the man and explained she was going to be their interpreter, and that he should say exactly what was on his mind.

The man let out an encouraged smile.

'*Ihu gi Na anya mara. I bi gburugburu ebe a?*' the man asked.

Oluchi grinned and swivelled to her cousin.

'He says you look unfamiliar. Where have you been hiding?'

Priscilla suspected those were not his exact words from the manner in which Oluchi spoke them.

'Tell him I have been away, and that I could also say the same of him. He looks unfamiliar.'

Priscilla saw the puckered brow on Oluchi's face; she obviously wasn't pleased with her reply.

Oluchi shifted her face to the man with a wide grin.

'*Okwru na I a mara mma okorobia, ma nnoo nzuzu maka iju ajuju out ahu.*'

The man's smiling countenance quickly changed into a frown and Priscilla whispered into her cousin's ear.

'Did you just tell him I said he is handsome but stupid for asking me such a question?'

'Don't worry aunty, I know how to handle men like this, all is well.'

Priscilla nodded and sat back, flashing the man a grin. 'Tell him I am awaiting his response.'

'So you do not know you're talking to the lady who just returned home from London,' Oluchi said to the man in Ibo in a scornful tone.

The man eyes widened. 'I didn't know,' he replied and went closer to Priscilla. 'No wonder your English is difficult to understand. Enjoy your night,' he bowed at her with a smile and walked away until his shadow was swallowed by the bonfire.

Priscilla watched sadly as the man walked away, realising her status meant she had become a scarecrow to men.

Oluchi burst into laughter. 'Aunty, if you had a car, a commoner as him won't think you so low as to be in his league.' She laughed again then started back to the bonfire.

While she detested how Oluchi had treated the young man, she found wisdom in her young cousin's words. Owning a car would increase her status in the town as well as ensure that only wealthy men would come seeking her hand, the kind of men that would improve her new lifestyle, and in so doing not expose her lie. The more she thought about it, the more it occurred to her that she couldn't afford to go broke now. What would people say when

Priscilla Igwe walked into a party and did not declare free food and drink for all? What would people say when Priscilla Igwe no longer donated sums of money towards town projects? What would people say if Priscilla no longer hosted family parties just for the fun of it? What would people say when they came to her family house and she could not provide money to pay for the goats and the drinks? She floundered over the obvious answers to her questions.

* * * *

Two months had gone by and Grandma's situation had not changed. She was neither dead nor alive. Priscilla often wondered if it was truly her who requested her family to return home or if her mother sold her that lie just so she could return home after a while of being away. Either way, it didn't seem like she would be leaving Anagara any time soon. This worried Priscilla because it meant she needed to find a solution to get more money to retain her status and respect. She sat beside Grandma pondering when Mama poked her head into the room.

'Priscilla, I am going out,' Mama announced. 'The rains are coming and I have to make sure our crops are ready for it,' she added and left.

Priscilla didn't look up at her mother, not interested in what she said because her mind was occupied with finding a solution to her problem. She picked up her phone and checked her account balance; it was less than half a million from two million naira. The money was a gift which came as a result of her honesty and now dishonesty was draining it from her. She looked at the door and Mama was gone. With urgency, she chased after her and caught up with her by the gate.

'Mama,' she called. 'I thought father on his dying bed made us swear never to farm in that land near *Akija* shrine until *Ndidichigbo* is dead?'

'Yes, and I haven't broken that promise. *Ndidichigbo* is still alive. If I am not mistaken, he should be close to four hundred and he doesn't look like he will be dying any time soon.'

Priscilla sighed as if imagining.

'We bought another piece of land to farm in.'

'Okay, I just wanted to be sure,' she replied with concealed exhilaration as she watched Mama leave. She walked back into the house knowing she had found the answer to the question she really intended to ask.

The wind threatened and the clouds went dark, but the rains didn't drop. At the fall of darkness in the depth of the night, Priscilla gripped the torch in her hand firmly as she dodged the tree branches that flung themselves at the call of the wind. She had arrived at *Ndidichigbo* sacred shrine. She looked at the entrance, heaved a determined sigh and entered walking backwards.

'*Ndidichigbo*, I...'

'Sometimes we think we know what we want but we actually don't know,' was the first statement *Ndidichigbo* said to her before she could greet him.

Priscilla paused, wondering how he knew why she had come before she even spoke a word. He is wise, she concluded.

'I am ready to do anything,' replied Priscilla, 'only money can solve my problem.'

Ndidichigbo grinned with confidence, which gave away the wrinkles around his mouth. 'Money comes and goes, my child, it is a vanity which denies one of happiness,' he paused and searched deeper into her eyes. 'Many have come just the way you have, and I know how it ended.'

'Baba, that is why I have come to you, wise one,' and in Ibo said, 'I know you'd help me regardless of what my people might say of you.'

'You say you're willing to do anything to make money?'

'Anything, *Ndidichigbo,* anything.'

'Okay,' he said to her with a straight face. 'It would require a sacrifice.'

'*Ndidichigbo*, I will buy all the fattest goats and cows and sacrifice them the way you direct me to. Just tell me the size to buy.'

'No, not a goat. I mean something bigger, someone, a person you really love to be precise.' Priscilla stopped moving, her gaze fixed on him, but he didn't budge, and it occurred to her he wasn't joking.

'I don't understand?'

Ndidichigbo said nothing further and she stood to leave, then he said 'On your way out, stare into the mirror for five minutes. If you choose to go on with the sacrifice, whoever you see is who you'd use to get wealth.'

Priscilla got to the entrance and stared into the mirror, and for the five minutes she looked, she saw nothing but her reflection.

* * * *

Grandma was coughing again and Priscilla stood to help her back to sleep. She sat next to her, unwilling to return to her room because since she returned from *Ndidichigbo's* shrine, all she could do was worry over not seeing anyone in the mirror aside from herself. *Ndidichigbo* was wise and could have only given her that exercise for a purpose; returning to him to say she saw no one aside herself would indicate she was unserious and incapable of going the mile to get what she wanted. She rose to stand in front of Grandma's mirror and stared at it for as long as she could, determined not to leave until she saw who *Ndidichigbo* wanted her to see. Her reflection was bold and beautiful, independent, daring, and youthful. She was reminded of how her mother often told her that she had a striking resemblance to her grandmother, in looks and in character.

'Your grandmother is a leading light in this town, and something tells me you would be too, wherever you go,' Priscilla recalled her mother saying to her just before she travelled.

In that instant it struck Priscilla who she was seeing in the mirror, the resemblance; it was her grandma. She staggered back in disarray as the picture became clear to her, then she shifted her gaze to Grandma.

'No way,' she whispered, trying hard to shake away the image.

Grandma was her best friend, her confidante and blood, no way was she going to sacrifice her for wealth even though she was at the tail end of her life and no one would suspect foul play. How could she live with herself afterwards? If Grandma's spirit didn't kill her, her conscience would.

She now understood what *Ndidichigbo* meant when he said money was vanity which denies one happiness. The more she thought about it, the more she cursed herself for even conceiving the idea in the first place of getting wealthy through ritual. Such thoughts were born out of laziness, desperation, greed, covetousness and dishonesty such as the one she had clung onto which had led her to this point.

At the break of dawn just as the sun rose, it dawned on Priscilla that something had changed in her within the two months she had returned home. She was slowly unbecoming the woman she intended to be, now lost, and living another identity. When the sun stood high in the sky and spread its rays across Anagara, she knew there was only one thing left to do, to re-identify herself, to build upon her strengths and weaknesses, to become the woman she had set out to be, one which the world couldn't resist, one which her family would be proud of.

'I have a confession to make,' announced Priscilla to her family who were gathering beneath the mango tree at the centre of their compound.

'Okay,' said one of her uncles, and they all paid attention.

She inhaled and exhaled, letting out a deep sigh pondering how to break the news to them, how to break herself free from a lie that was beginning to swallow her.

'Hurry up, some people need to hurry to the farm and their place of work,' Mama told her.

'I am not who you think I am,' said Priscilla.

They all stared at her, confused. Oluchi stepped forward to touch her, looked back to the others and shrugged.

'I am still the Priscilla Igwe you know. What I mean is that I have been lying to you all since I arrived. Actually, it started out as an innocent remark.' She shifted between their gazes and they all stood staring at her without any attempt to interrupt her confession. 'I wasn't in London as you all think, I was based in Lagos, hustling and driving a cab. A week before I returned home, an *oyibo* woman forgot a bag in my cab and when I returned it to her; she rewarded me with two million naira. That is what I've been spending.'

They all kept mute, looked each other in the eye, and as if planned, they all burst into loud laughter except for Oluchi, who was frowning. Mama stepped forward and put her arms around her daughter.

'Why is everyone laughing? I just told you that I have been lying,' Priscilla moaned.

'Priscilla, my dear child, truth is we all knew you weren't in London. But because you didn't correct the misinterpretation, who were we to correct it for you?' They all again erupted in laughter.

'So you people were bleeding me dry of my earnings and you knew?'

'No, Priscilla,' said her uncle. 'You were bleeding yourself. We thought you'd at least tell us, your family, the truth, but you didn't, so we joined you in living your lie.'

'At least I ate many goat meats,' someone said and they laughed again.

Priscilla raked her hand into her hair, at first angry at her family, then at herself. While it was easy to blame them for not correcting her, she herself was to blame for lying to them too.

'Your family will always love you regardless of who or what you are,' Mama said. 'Even if you lie to the world, lie to your family or those close to you, do not lie to yourself, 'because when you do, you are already dead.'

Priscilla burst into tears and everyone came around her in solace. 'Thank you,' she said with a snivelling voice. 'I will forever remember this lesson.'

'I can't believe this!' Oluchi shouted. 'How do I tell my friends that you have been telling us fake stories? Is your accent even real?'

'No. I had to practise it to keep up the act.'

'God! I will lose all the friends that I just made,' Oluchi cried as she walked away mumbling, and everyone laughed.

LOVE IN A TIME OF MASSACRE

To the fallen men of Iva valley, history shall forever engrave your names: Sunday Anyajodo, Obazu Mbezi, Livinus Okechukwuma – the machine operator from Ohi; Owerri. Okafor Ageni – an Udi tub man, Moses the machine operator from Mbutu, Nwalu the engineer driver from Anazi Bendi and 15 others.

Okafor started out at the break of dawn; he could wait no longer. The love of his life would leave later today and every moment with her counted. Today wasn't going to be momentary like other days when he defied Nna and Nne to sneak out under the moonlight just to be with her and be lost in her warm embrace –how he cherished those moments. He remembered the night Nne almost died due to his negligence; he was supposed to have watched her till Nna returned from the native healer with some herbal drugs, but no, he snuck out to be with his love. She meant everything to him. The mere thought of seeing her no more tortured his heart, troubled his soul and haunted his very existence. It was the reason why he was going to do what he intended to do. He'd damn all consequences, damn tradition – which hadn't helped in any way – and more importantly, damn his parents.

The atmosphere around Iva valley was serene and placid as usual. The morning dew which wets the flowers and plants had gone about its duty; now all the plants were dripping water from their morning bath. Everything was changing in Enugu, especially since the building of the Iva valley mine in 1917 after Udi coal mine was closed. One could guess the reason for the closure, but it didn't matter anymore.

The sun was beginning to rise; Okafor quickened his feet, his appointment was getting nigh and nothing in this world was going to make him miss it. Anything other than showing up under the mango tree which was planted at the heart of the town spelt doom, one which his heart would forever hold against him.

'*Ututu oma*' he greeted an older man whom he thought should have grey hairs as a result of his astuteness.

This was his sixth greeting and it was beginning to bore him. It was the consequence of knowing too many men and women, and their sons and daughters. He had Nna to blame for such popularity, one which got on his nerves.

'Okafor,' he heard a feminine voice call from a distance. He swivelled with a feigned smile plastered on his face, but not fast enough to see the face of whoever had called his name as his neck was stiffened by the many thoughts of his meeting with Onyinye. He kept his gaze on the person as she walked away, thinking she looked extraordinary from behind, then she turned and shot him a weird glance and turning away again, she was gone. There was something odd about her squint – it implied mockery, but he couldn't be sure. Did she know of his plans and mocked him because the idea in itself was foolery, and him a fool for thinking the gods would bind him with an abomination? Love is after all foolish.

His heart had gone ahead to carry out a reconnaissance under the mango tree to see if his love was there, patiently waiting for him, but he couldn't see clearly, the air hampering his sight. He wasn't bothered, love is blind. He had chosen the mango tree for its significance. Enugu was fast growing into a giant city increased infrastructure meant the city was standing at the dawn of a new era. Everything old about Enugu had been destroyed but for some reason the famous mango tree stood, and it was there lovers met. It was rumoured that before *Amadioha* left for his sanctuary, he and his lover exchanged loving vows one last time under that same mango tree. The whole town know what happens when lovers meet under the tree, a sacred encounter.

The morning was now in full bloom. Empty roads wanting wear had feet striding to and from their homes and local working places. The cocks played around in roo having no one to wake from their slumber. Dawn was still and peaceful, but in the stillness of the morning, there was something odd; no miners had been seen around – neither Nna nor his friends had made away for the mines. This wasn't normal for them – they hardly ever waited that long to head to the mines, they mostly raced against the rising sun and they always won.

The coal mine was of importance to the town and Nigeria as a country, especially during the war, and continued to be vital in the rebuilding of infrastructure by the post-war labour government, who sought to maximise output to pay off its debt to the United States of America. In 1943, with inflation raging, they had been called upon to make up the shortfall in the British coalfields caused by the war. It was nothing new to them that they had saved the British arse and had been led to believe their sacrifices would create a better world, whilst their bosses were planning for a future that didn't exist.

'Okafor!' called someone; it was the voice of an elder. The tone gave the voice away before he even looked, it was Nna's close friend, Makuochukwu.

'Good morning, sir,' Okafor greeted him with modesty, hoping it wouldn't betray his intended action. It was said that the elderly were so wise that they could sense evil or abomination in a person's voice.

It was probably one of those lies told to children to make them desist from lying.

'How I wish the morning is as good as you have greeted,' he said, sounding disconcerted.

This time, it was the other way around, the texture of his voice suggesting something was wrong, urgent and raw, but it was impossible to detect what that was. Discerning it was probably for the elderly alone.

'Is your father still at home?'

'Yes, I left him—'

'When you get home, remind him today's date in case he has forgotten,' he said in a hurry and left.

'He forgets a lot of things these days,' Okafor replied in a low voice and chortled.

The mango tree was in sight, but not Onyinye, she was nowhere near. He hurried beneath the tree and looked around, assuming she was watching him. She had been here, he was sure; her pleasant scent of ardour saturated the air, but not her physical company.

How could she have left in the hour he had hoped for the most, leaving him in odious despair? He found his feet; he was going to walk home the same way he had come, angry at her, disappointed at love.

'I didn't think you'd come again,' he heard a soothing voice from behind him say.

Okafor stopped; he knew very well the voice and could recognise it any given time and day. It had only been two weeks, but those weeks were enough to keep glued to his ears the rhythmic voice of an angel in human form. He smiled and turned to her.

'I'm sorry I took so much time getting here.'

He embraced her, tightly, gripping the curves of her waist, seduced by the edges of her nipples. He had missed that feeling, but not anymore, not after his intentions were made known.

'My father said we'd leave before the sun set. What he had hoped to do wasn't productive,' her eyes fell in disappointment. 'I'm sorry,' she echoed in a low voice.

Considering her background, it wasn't surprising nobody dared to associate with her kind; it was a segregation only love could break, would break.

'I know,' he finally said. 'I wish it wasn't so.'

'I'm just glad our love blossomed while it lasted. Goodbye Okafor, I'll miss you.'

Okafor didn't let her words end when he grabbed her by the arm.

'No, I'm not giving up on you, I have a plan,' he retorted, discerning the look in her eyes, a mixture of hope and fear.

After a long pause of internal denial, she said. 'I hope it's not what I think it is?'

He said nothing but squeezed her hands. She was right, he was going to do what she feared he would.

She pulled away her hands.

'No, it can't work. My history has decided my fate. I am an Osu and would never be accepted by your people.' There was a long pause, to bury the pain in her voice, and then she added, 'I am cursed.'

'Fate, you say. I refuse to be driven by fate, or do you not know that men sometimes are masters of their own fate? I have decided to be master over mine.'

'Your people forbids it. It's a tradition that has—'

'I do not care about a tradition that was founded upon greed and hate by our ancestors. Tell me, why should we hate another fellow man just because he was a slave? Were we not all once slaves to the whites? And who sold us? It was the Blacks who sold Blacks.' He let out a long sigh. 'The bedrock of our tradition is laid upon thorny grounds. We cannot continue to hate people because their ancestral parents were slaves to the gods.' He paused and heaved another sigh, uncertain if he should let the next words out of his mouth. 'Sometimes one doubts if the gods exist.'

'Don't let the gods strike you this moment for blasphemy.' Onyinye put her hands over his mouth. She searched his eyes; he meant every word he said. It was clear he had within the period of their meeting decided his fate. She feared the worse. Two weeks was too short a time for a man to fall so crazy in love that he was willing to go against his parents and tradition, yet, she couldn't deny the pleasure of hearing a man declare he was going to fight the entirety of an unfound tradition for her sake – for the sake of their love.

'I know, but what can we do? Our forefathers made these laws, we can't disobey them.'

'But we can question them,' he retorted, 'as well as anything that isn't logical or is against the benefit of another fellow man. I do not respect such authority.'

There was a strained silence in the air; Okafor drew her close into his arms. He could see the fear in her eyes, sense the worry in her thoughts, of how his love for her was pushing him away from his tribe, away from tradition, and from his conservative parents. What she didn't know was that he had always hated some of the traditional laws, chiefly those such as an Igbo man being forbidden to marry an

Osu because their forefathers were slaves.

'All I want to know is, will you marry me?'

Onyinye's breath died away.

'If you had the chance, would you?' Okafor asked again.

She floundered in abrupt silence as she withdrew away from his grasp. She looked away to think about it even though there was nothing to think about. She let out a deep sigh, complemented by a long minute of smiling that seemed like it would never end.

'Yes,' she said.

'Hmmm!?'

'Over and over again, I would say yes.'

His heart froze for five seconds before it began to beat again. His eyes remained wide, and unable to steady his smile, he embraced her tightly, disinclined to let go.

'Now I can go home and tell Nna my intention, to marry you.'

Onyinye let out a wide grin, but her eyes gave her uneasiness away.

'There's no need to worry. I do not care about the outcome of my telling them,' he said, 'it is just a formality out of respect. I'd get married to you regardless.'

'Okay.'

She didn't want to hear those words; it meant he would be disobeying his family, his tradition and any other obstacle to his decision to marry an Osu, but she loved that he said them.

Okafor left for home straight away, all through the journey thinking about how he'd break the news to Nna and Nne. It would break Nne's heart but she would eventually come round, all good mothers do. He had a feeling Nna would forbid such abomination, marrying an Osu into the family. That was insult enough.

* * * *

'*Amadioha* strike your stupid mouth,' Nna flared up.

He was already dressed for work, but delayed a little to treat his son's growing madness. 'You will not bring shame into my household, I forbid you.'

'It's too late, Nna, I already asked her to marry me and she said yes.'

'Fool! What do you expect her to say if not yes? Is she not but an Osu who will dive into the naïve and senseless arms of a true son of this land who doesn't know his left from right.'

Okafor couldn't tell if that was a statement or question, yet either of the two made no difference to him.

'I forbid you to insult my household, my ancestors and our tradition,' Nna concluded.

At that, he set out for the mines, casting a long accusing gaze at Nne. He had accused rather than suggested that she had had a hand in her son's budding stupidity.

'Have patience with him, you know how stubborn your father can be,' Nne said, breaking her son's angry gaze at his father as he walked away. But her words were a failed attempt to persuade Okafor, who didn't want to hear what she had to say. His heart was laden with rage and determination. He would go against everything Nna had mentioned and would build his own legacy, one not built on baseless traditions.

'I've always told you to not be harsh with him,' Nne continued. 'You both have the same adamant nature.'

'Nne, that doesn't change anything. I am his son, he should be considerate. He mustn't always be too rigid.'

'Are you sure she is who you want to marry?'

'I am very sure, Nne, and I would—' he paused.

An idea hit him. Reanimated, he came to a decision. 'I am going to meet Nna at the mines, he must agree to my marriage.'

He walked away hearing Nne in the distance pleading, 'Please don't expose our troubles. Once the wind gets hold of it, it's no longer for our ears only.'

* * * *

Okafor got to the mines but met a different scenario from what it used to be. He should have suspected; he knew something was wrong but what he was seeing wasn't part of it. Nna sat by the entrance of the end of the mine, and reaching him meant passing the other men but he feared the hostility before him. He decided to stand and watch from a distance. Nna had a piece of red cloth around his arm, as did the other striking miners; it marked solidarity.

He didn't think the miners would take the strike seriously, as they feared the British. To not go against the British was wisdom, yet there they were, all in unison for the first time in a long time, kicking against their poor working conditions and poor remuneration, especially having worked their arses off to save the British. He had often heard Nna complain to Nne about the backlog of money owed them during the time of casualization, which was known as rostering. It was later declared illegal, but some eighteen miners on the first of November were sacked following a work to rule. That was surely the main cause for their striking action, it was justifiable.

'This is fearlessness against oppression,' he said to himself with a constant delighted nod.

Nna stood to go shake hands with Okwudili Ojiyi, his coworker, whom a Mr T. Yates had slapped some years ago. Okwudili did one of the bravest things by suing the British man for assault and to the town's surprise, he won. Yates was prosecuted and penalised. Both men stood on the sidelines discussing something which could well be related to their strike action as they were making gestures towards their fellow workers around.

Okafor learnt from one of the miners striding the field that the management had opted to remove the mines, fearing the growing agitation for independence was a hidden motivation for their strike. For that reason, the white man in the centre, holding his gun firm and fierce – Briton superintendent police captain F. S. Philip – alongside two others, had been sent to oversee the local police removing the mines since the workers refused to help. He could perceive Philip was on edge all the while, the way he held onto his gun, his bewildered gaze, suggested he saw the miners as a threat. He simply saw them through the same lens as black skins were seen –primitive, savage and hysterical natives doing dangerous dances and squealing incomprehensible noises. To him, they were nothing but dangerous Black men poised to attack.

Okafor didn't want to forget why he came. Nothing was going to distract him, not even Captain Philip's apprehensive silent gesture. He was about to make his way across to the other half of the field where Nna was talking with Okwudili, when Ebere, his closest friend, grabbed him.

'Where do you think you're going?' Ebere queried, his eye all over the mine.

'To talk to my father,' Okafor shot back.

'Can you not see trouble looms right ahead of you? What is so important that can't wait till he returns home?'

'He doesn't want me to marry the woman I love.'

'Anulika!? But they've never had a problem with her as a future wife for you!'

'No, not her. I fell in love with a girl from Anambra and I intend to marry her, but Nna refuses because she's an Osu, which is not fair.' There was pain in his voice as he recollected.

Ebere stared at him in silence then burst into an uncontrolled laughter.

'Nothing is fair in love and war, my friend.'

'Love and war! Who said anything about war?'

'What is in front of you?' asked Ebere. Okafor looked. 'I sense today will end in blood and tears. It's not like it's the first time the British have attacked us with our country looking the other way. I'm sure of one thing though; this singular action today will serve as motivation for the Zik movement for independence.'

'I expect you to give me advice about the trouble of my love life and you're telling me about the miners' strike!? I don't bloody care what happens here,' Okafor retorted in a tone of arrogance.

'There are some wars that can't be won, except at a steep price.'

'I'm talking about love and you're telling me about war. Please be focused!'

'I am. You're about to fight a war.'

'With who!?'

'With your parent, and with a long-standing culture. Do you really want to go that route because of love that could as well be blind?'

Okafor for the first time paused to think about the severity of his actions and the domino effect it'd cause. He looked across the field, his eyes settled on Captain Philip's gun. He shook his head and started to speak, but Ebere gestured that he stop.

'Think about it – what life can't change, death will.'

'What does that mean?'

Ebere said nothing further.

The hour was clocking noon and the sun coming out in its full glory The workers were becoming tired of their protest but still maintaining their stance, raising their voices and moving in circles. Captain Philip didn't see it that way; he must have supposed it was looming danger. He became hysterical and gave the order to shoot, himself pointing his revolver at Anyajodo, who had recently got married. Before anyone could say Jack Robinson, he fired the first shot, killing Sunday Anyajodo. Other officers began to shoot randomly.

'What is happening?' asked Agani, who rushed out into the rising chaos.

He too was shot. He'd get his answer in the grave.

There was pandemonium, miners running helter-skelter, and the gunshots, mostly misfired, went into the backs of many, sending good folks to the ground. Then the gunshots stopped.

In the stillness after the shots came a shout, 'I surrender.' It was the voice of Emmanuel, an injured blacksmith. 'Take me to the hospital,' he begged.

'I don't care,' Captain Philip shouted back, then he and his band made away after much havoc had been wreaked.

'Okafor!' Nna shouted.

Nna was lying at the edge of the mines, injured too. Okafor took him by the arm, helped him home. The walk was silent. Okafor was glad that now Nna would agree with him in what he had always said: '*The British are killing us*', but importantly, this event would help change Nna's course of reasoning and let him marry Onyinye. Death has a way of making men see life differently, to know that life is but a cloth we wear that will one-day fade and wear off. There is no law or philosophy too rigid and dogged that cannot be changed.

* * * *

Nne was cleaning Nna's bullet wound; it had merely grazed him. Luck must have kept him for a purpose.

'Their action must not go unpunished – they should pay. They will pay.'

Nna's voice was becoming fierce, like he had a plan. Nne touched a part of his shoulder and he screamed in pain. He was injured there too.

'Nna, I hope now you see I was always right when I said the British are killing us?'

'They are, yes they are,' his voice drowning in the pain of his injury. 'By now, Nnamdi Azikiwe must have heard the news and have begun making plans of an attack.'

Nne directed an unfriendly look at her husband and he knew what she meant.

'Or a strike back of some sort,' he corrected. 'But it has become clear Nigeria as a nation must fight for our independence from this modern slavery we've found ourselves in.'

Okafor nodded, not really caring at this point who must fight for what. He cared that Nna had agreed with him on something.

'It's the same way I'm right about marrying the woman I love.'

Nna ignored him, more concerned about his injuries. He probably didn't hear the words clearly until he paused after a botched attempt to move his leg. The words rang and caused a sting in his ear.

'I already said no and nothing will change that. What is wrong with you people? First the British bring an abomination to my home town and now my son wants to bring an abomination to my household. The gods forbid,' he gesticulated.

Nne pressed his shoulder again and his face lit with quiet scream, curves of pain shaping around his mouth, eye prickling in livid dismay. He had spoken and wouldn't change his mind for anything. That was clear.

Nne finished cleaning his wound, moved her gaze between the two men in her life. It was easy to know what she was thinking.

'What about Anulika,' she asked. 'You had once said you would marry her. Didn't you?'

'It's you people that wanted me to marry her... and that was before I met Onyinye.'

'That is her name? Onyinye! I forbid that name in this house,' Nna barked. 'You want to disgrace mine and my father's name so that the whole town can mock me? Never! Not in this lifetime.'

A kind of silence erupted, one that nobody spoke after. There was conflict in Okafor's thought, pain in his heart; Nna would, for his own selfishness, prevent him from marrying the woman he had come to love. Who cared about what people would say of his actions? They were his after all, and not theirs. What annoyed him more was that the same people who spread rumours committed the same or worse crimes in secret, most likely in a different manner, but still the same. Hypocrites, that's what they were, hypocrites!

Okafor jumped to his feet, 'I'd rather die than live and not marry the woman I love because of some stupid tradition created by selfish men.'

At that, he started away.

'Let him go,' he heard Nna warn Nne. 'He must think death is child's talk.'

Nne obeyed and continued to tend her husband's wound.

Okafor dashed to the back of the compound, clouded by love and anger. He had decided he'd take his own life; his death would make Nna and the elders learn from their mistakes. He tied a rope above the tree branch nearest to his height, and slid his neck into the loop. He would have preferred another method of death, one without struggles and pain, but suicide had a meaning in Igbo land. He swung himself forward, kicking away the stool he had stood on, then he began to choke, breathless, legs dangling above the ground. He could feel his life draining by the seconds, and the tides of his past life roving before his eyes. He managed to smile a smile of death, happy he hadn't lived a life of regret. His legs had stopped dangling, his hands about to fall lifeless, when boom, he fell to the ground.

'Harrrrhhh!' he gasped back to life, holding his leg in pain.

He looked up at the tree; the branch the rope was tied to had broken. Maybe fate was talking to him, telling him that death didn't solve anything, that there were other ways. He decided he would be master over his own fate and run away with Onyinye before the sun had set.

He packed his bag and peeped at Nna, who was still mumbling something to Nne. He was going to run, do the abominable and defy the so-called gods. He would first visit Anulika one last time, he at least owed her that much.

He took one last look at his parents. Nne was applying native medicine made from leaves to Nna's wound. One thing was sure, Nna would every day look at his scar and remember November 18, 1949, the day Iva valley lost so many men in one fell swoop to a massacre, and the same day he lost a son who ran from home because he fell in Love in a Time of Massacre.

DECEIVED

Miranda Irrua placed her knuckles against the door and breathed deep, deep enough to push her breast against the wooden door. The air burst out of her as she wrapped her hand around the doorknob. She was ready and determined that tonight everything ended, and nothing would change her mind. She touched her bag to feel the knife in it, then attempted to open the door, but it was locked from the inside. She knocked again.

'A few seconds,' Charles shouted.

The sound of his voice at that moment irritated her, everything about him did, or she forced herself to believe it did, down to the idea of his existence. His sweet innocent face was a façade, she always convinced herself. She needed no other proof; he was guilty of having murdered Lisa. That was what the letter said, and vengeance would be hers tonight in one fell swoop.

It shouldn't have been Miranda to carry out the job tonight; Stan, the killer she had hired, had ghosted her. If it hadn't been for him, she and Charles would never have met or got this personal. Her several attempts to reach Stan had been futile, he had just disappeared. Charles must have killed him – he truly is a killer, she thought. It was why she had bought out the apartment just opposite him to keep an eye on his activities. It was why she pretended to be friends – maybe a little more than a friend – and now she was this close to avenging Lisa's death. Lisa was her responsibility, her younger sister. After their mother died, she had sworn upon her tomb that she would become a mother to Lisa. Now she lived day to day burdened by the discomfort of being a colossal failure for having broken her oath. She recalled she was in a brothel about to go down on a client when her phone had rung; it was Lisa calling, but Miranda didn't pick up. That was the last time anyone heard or saw Lisa until the letter showed up on her doorstep.

Lisa had been her only chance to take responsibility, to prove she could be responsible for someone or something, but Charles had taken that chance from her, and he was going to pay. She swore it.

'Sorry for--' Charles stopped his sentence halfway on opening the door, staring at Miranda dumbfounded.

Miranda knew the thoughts roving around his mind as he ran his eyes over her silky red gown. She had been specific in her choice of gown and colour, knowing his weakness for seductive red apparel, which ripped his reasoning from limb to limb.

'Please, do come in,' he gestured, mesmerised. 'I am making dinner. Your favourite.'

He let out a smile and dashed to the kitchen, but his cologne remained. Miranda looked about; the sitting room was put in order, lit with red candles and the walls dressed with bewitching paintings. His attention to details was a thing she loved about him, his every gesture titillating and romantic. It was how he stole her heart the first night she came to his house, which led to their first kiss. It was a mistake that should have ended as soon as it began, but every time their lips brushed against each other, her urge to resist his charm was defeated. Instead, she gripped him tighter and moaned in ecstasy. He tore his shirt, pinned her back against the wall with rage and urgency, unleashing his long years of galling chastity inside her, and she embraced his ravishing hunger. After their unbridled lovemaking, he rolled over to the other side of the bed staring at her contentedly, his eyes laden with admiration, his breath oozing with the desire for more. Miranda looked away and swore in silence,

'Tonight will never repeat itself.'

They'd had several of the same nights since then, and he had electrified her every single time.

'Tonight will be different,' she assured herself, shaking her mind off the previous nights. 'Tonight it ends.'

Charles returned, walking into the room with a broad smile and Miranda cursed beneath her breath, 'God! Stop it! Please not that smile.'

His shirt was unbuttoned, and her eyes played on the hairs spread across his expansive chest.

'Hey,' he called.

He locked his hand with hers, lifted and planted a kiss on it, while his breath tickled the hairs on her skin. He withdrew, hunting her face with a voracious gaze, so that when he leaned forward and let his lips linger on hers, breathless, she clutched onto her bag to be reminded of the purpose of tonight's visit.

'How was your day?' he asked, his eyes wandering over her dress.

'Fine, but was boring as usual. Yours?' she asked in one breath, hoping her voice wouldn't betray her intent as her heart began to beat fast. She broke away from his hold and stepped back. 'Is the food ready?'

'It is. I will go and serve.'

He flashed her a grin as he started for the kitchen and Miranda let out a sigh of relief. It occurred to her how easy it was to conceive of the idea of killing, but actually to make the kill required courage, and the little courage she had mustered he was taking away with his quixotic gestures. It was a difficult job Stan did, she thought. Money seemed like a good motivation at least. What was her motivation?

Vengeance, she nodded. She grabbed her purse and started after him with a gritty countenance.

She walked in to see Charles dishing spaghetti into a curved plate, unaware he was no longer alone in his marbled kitchen.

'It's now or never,' she convinced herself. 'A life for a life.'

Her heartbeat accelerated as she unzipped her bag, edging her way behind him. She reached into the bag eager to pull out the knife and drive it into him. That way, she wouldn't be driven by guilt when she saw the fading eyes of the man who was willing to lay the world at her feet, and satisfied her lust better than any man she had ever known. She ran her hand across the blade. It aroused a cold longing in her, a desire to feel his warmth inside her before she stabbed him cold.

Charles turned around and almost dropped the plate on seeing her. 'Jeez! You scared me.' He took in her position and moved his head back. 'Are you okay?'

Miranda nodded, slowly withdrawing her hand from her bag. She feigned a smile, looking from side to side and wondering if he had known she was behind him all along.

'I know that feeling,' Charles said, laying the plate of food on the counter. 'I sometimes feel the same way too.'

'What way?' asked Miranda, confused.

'Like I am being watched.'

'Being watched?' Miranda winced. 'Like spied upon?'

Charles nodded.

Shit! Miranda cursed beneath her breath and took a step back. What if he had known her intentions from the start, but was simply goading her to this final moment, so he could kill her claiming self-defence and walk scot-free after committing two murders? 'Why do you think so?' she found the boldness to ask, determined to avenge her sister's murder even if it led to her own.

'Every now and then I turn around, it's like someone is watching me, studying me or maybe plotting against me,' he said with dread in his voice.

He is good, Miranda thought, he deserves a movie award. What if he was behind Stan's disappearance? her mind continued to boggle. He was more dangerous than he appeared. It was now or never, to drive the knife into his torso and fulfil her promise; to end the life of the man who had taken her sister's life. Her hands began to tremble as she thought to reach into her bag again and grab the knife.

'Are you okay? You look distressed. Or is there something you want to tell me?'

'Why would you ask me that?'

Charles winced. 'I don't know. Why do you think I would you ask that?'

'You tell me,' she shot back.

'I don't know. I mean you've been behaving unusually since you walked in. I kissed you but you didn't respond like you normally would. You've been holding onto that bag since you arrived, and now you're looking around like you are searching for or expecting something.'

Fuck it! she whispered to herself. He knows! If she was going to do it, it had to be now while he still played dumb.

'Miranda,' he said, moving closer to her, 'I know it's you who have been watching me. You're a jealous lover.' He broke into a smile.

'Jealous lover!?' Miranda recoiled. 'Since when did we become lovers?'

'We've been having sex, haven't we?'

'Sex a couple of times doesn't make us lovers.'

'Good fucking sex does,' he said and smiled.

Miranda didn't smile back. She hated that he was becoming too attached, and his attraction was so infectious that she was beginning to break her own rule by mistaking good sex for love. Her affairs with the previous men in her life had always being brusque, a brief match-flare that died as soon as it was lit. She always believed it was foolish women who found love through sex; as it turned out, she had been foolish since her first night with Charles, but denied it with the excuse that she was doing it for a good cause.

'Men find sex through love,' said Miranda in a defeated tone. 'How come you're finding love through sex? I thought that is what women do.'

'Perhaps I am a woman and do not know,' said Charles and Miranda chuckled. 'But you've charmed me into loving you, and no, it's not just because of the sex, though I must admit you make me hungry where most you satisfy. It is everything about you that thrills me.'

Miranda's heart melted and she leaned in to kiss him. Slowly, she withdrew her lips with a fixed ambivalent gaze at Charles, and when she opened her mouth to speak, silent tears trickled down her face.

'Hey,' Charles said with a tender voice. 'Don't cry. You don't have to say a word. You don't have to say you love me too.'

He cast his arms around her and held her close to his chest. Miranda slid into his embrace trembling, in tears.

'It's all right, baby,' said Charles reassuringly. 'It's all right.'

Miranda nodded. Her hands behind him, she opened her bag and brought out the knife unbeknownst to him, lifting it to his nape, threatening to drive it in. She closed her eyes, heaved a sigh, and when she opened them, she looked straight into his eyes. 'I'm sorry.' She made to drive the knife down-- and then the doorbell rang and she paused. She remained still for a few seconds with Charles in her embrace. She made to strike again and the doorbell rang for the second time and then repeatedly. She slid back the knife into the bag as Charles pulled away.

'I should get that, or the person won't leave,' Charles teased. Miranda nodded. 'Don't move,' he said hurrying for the door. 'We'll pick up where we left off.'

She wiped her tears, relieved and sad at the same time. The night wasn't going to plan, and tonight was all she had. Her flight left in the middle of the night for good, and she wasn't going to leave without avenging her sister's death regardless of the amorous throbs her heart beat for her sister's murderer. A life for a life, she reminded herself.

A minute after and Charles was yet to return. A surprising silence filled the house.

'Charles!' she called but there was no answer. 'Charles,' she called, hurrying into the sitting room, worried. 'Charles, are you…?' she came to a sudden halt, staring at Charles and a face she knew only too well standing by the door. 'Lisa!' she called in a fading voice, then collapsed to the floor.

Little by little Miranda opened her eyes, her face wet from the water that had been sprinkled over her. Charles was standing over her with folded arms and a grim face, then shifted his gaze to Lisa who stood opposite him, and Miranda followed his eyes. She jumped back up, reached for her bag and pointed the knife at Lisa, moving backwards to Charles to protect him.

'Stay away from us.' She turned to Charles, 'She is not real, she is a ghost.'

'She is your younger sister, Lisa. And she has told me everything,' Charles said in a melancholy voice.

Miranda shifted her gaze to Lisa, who flashed her a smile. 'Hello big sis,' she opened her arms for an embrace but Miranda recoiled.

'The Lisa I know is dead. You're not her!'

'Will you please drop the knife and listen to her?' Charles fired with annoyance.

'No!' Miranda shot back. 'This is a ghost.'

'Look at the resemblance.'

Miranda looked back at her sister; aside from getting bigger, she was still the Lisa she knew. Plump with a round face, a charming smile and a striking resemblance they shared with their late mother.

'No, I don't believe you,' she shook her head.

'Look out the window,' Lisa said. 'Maybe you'll believe me.'

Miranda moved her gaze to Charles and he gestured to the window. Miranda moved slowly to the window, her knife still pointed at Lisa. She peered past the curtain and saw a huge dark man standing by her car. She looked closer and winced.

'Is that Stan!?'

'Yes. He didn't disappear with your money like you might have assumed, I paid him off,' said Lisa.

'You paid... okay wait! What is going on here!? You're supposed to be dead. Let's start with that.'

'I know but, I've missed you,' said Lisa, and she ran to embrace

Miranda, who still stood shocked. 'I really missed you.'

It was really Lisa, in flesh and blood. Miranda welcomed Lisa into her arms, amidst laughter and shock. 'I can't believe this. H-how have you been? Wh-where have you been? How are you alive?' she asked all at once. 'The letter said he killed you.' Miranda turned to Charles and flashed him a sorry gaze then turned back to her sister.

'That is what I wanted you to believe,' replied Lisa, 'it was all a plan.' She turned to Charles. 'You were both pawns in my plot.'

Miranda wiped away her tears and said, 'Now I am confused.'

Charles leaned against the wall as Lisa cleared her throat in a bid to resolve her sister's confusion. He too needed to hear the story a second time.

'After mother died and you swore to become my mother to protect me, believe me, sister, nothing made me happier than that. But I wasn't pleased with the lifestyle you chose in order to be able to keep your promise. I didn't want to be the reason you sold your body. I decided the only way to give you a purpose was to make you think I was dead.'

'So you faked your death in a letter and made me swear to avenge you,' Miranda said in realisation.

'Yes,' Lisa nodded.

Charles frowned, yet found himself nodding at her brilliance.

'Are you crazy?' Miranda asked, anger replacing confusion. Lisa's face dropped. She didn't seem to understand where her sister's joy of seeing her again had vanished to.

'And how did he come into the picture?' Miranda pointed at Charles.

'I told a friend of my intention and she pointed out Charles, said he would be the perfect bait. He is a simpleton,' she turned to Charles, 'not in a bad way.'

Charles scowled.

'But he is a good person, lonely, the kind of man to offer the world at your feet if he feels you're deserving of it.'

Charles let out a smile, but when Miranda turned to him, he frowned.

'Are you crazy?' Miranda asked again, her voice increasing in tempo. 'I could have killed an innocent person to avenge you!' Miranda said, furious.

'No Miranda,' Lisa said, taking her hands. 'I know you couldn't, and that you would hire Stan. I reached him first and paid him off.'

Miranda held the back of her head. She was too upset to think.

'Lisa, that was a gamble. I could have killed him!'

Charles eye widened.

'To try to kill him, you'd have to get close to him. I knew he would charm you before you could strike. But now, I'm not sure who charmed who. You two look good together, I must admit.'

'I guess it's you who has been watching me then?' Charles asked Lisa.

'Me and Stan actually. We kept an eye on you two in case things were about to get out of hand, like tonight.'

Charles slid onto the sofa, turning his head away. 'Alas! I have been deceived by love's smart camouflage.'

Lisa reached to hold Miranda, but Miranda shrugged, "Don't touch me".

"Why would you fake your own death? Do you have any idea how much I cried?! Do you have any idea how it felt like blaming myself night after night for something that did not even happen?"

"But I just told you why I did it! I thought you'd see things from my perspective" Lisa retorted. "What perspective, for goodness's sake?! I was this close, this close to killing an innocent man that had nothing to do with either of us because you framed him!" Miranda was full on shouting now. She was dumbfounded. She couldn't believe her sister had thought to do something so stupid and dangerous.

"It was to give you a purpose!"

"Give me a purpose?" Miranda asked incredulously, "if you were so uncomfortable with the way I chose to provide for you, couldn't you have talked to me about it? Instead, you decided to... to do this!?"

Charles had heard enough. He almost died in his own home in the hands of a woman he trusted because she thought he killed her sister.

"Both of you are crazy. Leave my house" Charles said walking to the door and opening it.

Miranda tried to apologise. She wanted him to see things from her view, but Charles wasn't having it. She knew it was irrational of her to ask someone she almost killed to listen to what she has to say. She picked up her bag and saw herself out.

'I know this is all crazy, but I think my sister likes you,' Lisa said to Charles. 'If you could forgive...'

Charles pointed outside through the door, and Lisa shut her mouth.

In all the possible scenarios Lisa had cooked up in her mind about the possible reactions her sister would have when she finally came clean, this wasn't one of them. Her intention for her sister was good, but only now have she realised she went about it the wrong way. She heaved a sad sigh and ran after Miranda. She has a sister's forgiveness to beseech.

DIARY OF A BLACK IMMIGRANT

WHEN IN DOUBT, FUCK. At first watch, I took to heart Al Pacino's words from the movie *Scent of a Woman*, but nothing about moving to the United Kingdom was doubtful for me until it was. I arrived at Heathrow airport stunned at the structural mesh and the working system they had in place; everything was done with a sheer sense of simplicity and speed. On stepping out into the open, I was welcomed by the whooshing coldness that swept the air.

'Shit!' I said with a shivering voice then exhaled, rubbing my palms against each other. I noticed a smoke-like vapour escape my mouth and my eyes popped wide, amazed. I exhaled again, this time longer, and so was the vapour. 'Holy shit!!' I chuckled with delight like Jerry did when he had just found cheese against Tom's wish. This, I concluded, would be the best feeling that would go into my mental moments of ecstasy.

As I started for the train station, I kept remembering Phoebe's experience of how she had missed her train stop and ended up in another city. It was over a year ago she told me that story, yet, I couldn't stop finding it funny, and as I was about to take a train for the first time in the UK, I wanted to be able to boast on a call to Phoebe about how I didn't end up like her. I boarded the train. It was my second train experience, but it felt like my first – I wanted it to be my first. I stopped at Liverpool Street as Ben, my friend from undergraduate days, had instructed. In a bid to catch the next train to Colchester, I took the escalator as directed by a bloke, then ended up underground. I looked around and shook the feeling of being lost; I wasn't going to be a Phoebe.

'Good afternoon,' I greeted an officer in a yellow reflective jacket trifling with a blonde bobby.

He turned to me with a smile and said, 'How can I help you, mate?' but I thought I saw at the corner of his eyes a wisp of anger for disrupting what seemed like philandering.

'I am trying to get a train to Colchester.' I mirrored his grin.

'Okay mate,' he began to direct me, but I could barely hear what he said. My guess was he was in a hurry to dismiss me.

'Thank you.' I went in the direction he pointed but ended up underground again. I took the next train and stopped at the next train stop; it was the same stop I had earlier stopped at, only this time, I was standing at the opposite side of the tracks. I took the stairs up and found myself at Liverpool Street station. I hadn't enough time to take in the significant white-clean structure which was busy with people of different colour and race. I met a guy in a reflective jacket and asked him the direction to catch my train. He took my ticket and rolled his eyes over it.

'You're past your time, you'll have to pay a hundred pounds' late fee.'

I could tell from his voice and his facial structure he was from Eastern Nigeria, though his native tongue was drowned with a quarter-baked British accent. 'Train to Colchester is at line fourteen,' he said in a disappointed voice. I looked at the instruction board hanging over his head, which said line eleven.

'Thank you.' I took back the ticket and started for my train, thinking to myself, '*This one be wan use me do maga sha!*'

I arrived in Colchester and got to experience first-hand the widespread joke of how the whites do not mind going naked during summer, when I saw a tiny ray of sun and ran towards it. It was a ray of warm hope.

Ben arrived, welcomed me, and we took a taxi to be able to carry my luggage to his place. Eager to spend my first pounds, I paid the taxi fare from the fifty-pound-note lying in my wallet. Now, I felt like a Londoner. I planned to tell Yinka, on our next phone conversation, to respect me, because I now spent pounds and he naira. I told Yinka this during a video call, he called me a *werey* and laughed me to scorn. I laughed too.

'Stay here and rest while I go to work,' Ben told me on arriving at his room in a shared apartment. He was a care worker who went from house to house attending to the elderly.

'Nah, I will join you,' I said, wanting to explore the city and suck in the *oyinbo* air. As we walked, he explained to me how the UK system was designed to make life easy for people to live, crimes were not common, and if one was caught committing a crime, it was assumed it was intentional. He informed me that the assumption we had about white people abandoning their aged parents to be taken care of by strangers was wrong. The government through care organisations pays professionals to take care of the elderly, he told me, and their children are supportive and available for them. He made me understand how the whites believed in professionalism, and only experts in a particular field were approved to take on duties in the said field.

'I hope there is regular light here?' I asked aboard a bus. Ben laughed. He looked at me and laughed harder.

'By light you mean electric power supply?' he asked.

I nodded, slowly. He laughed again.

'Are you joking or are you serious?' he asked, his countenance full of curiosity.

I wasn't sure how to reply. It was an innocuous question. The bus we rode in had driven past a number of stores of which none had their light bulbs on, and this, I thought, was odd compared to the stores in Nigeria whose light bulbs were left on anytime there was power supply. That night, on returning to his place, he turned on the light switch, placed his hand on my shoulder and laughingly said, 'My friend, in this country, there is always light. No shaking.'

I took a night bus to my final destination, Glasgow in Scotland, and arrived at the break of dawn. The cold in Colchester was warm compared to that of Glasgow. As I got to learn, Glasgow was a city of four seasons in one day. Without presage, rain would shower down, and unlike in Nigeria where the slightest drops of rain drove people into hiding, otherwise in a matter of minutes you'd be drenched in the heavy downpour, here, people went about their duties because the rain – however sometimes windy – was light and somewhat friendly. Everything in the United Kingdom was about timing; the buses wouldn't wait a minute later than their departure times, the trains too, and missing your time could involve waiting another ten or thirty minutes for your next ride. It was no wonder people walked in a hurry.

That morning, with my luggage, I combed the streets in search of the bus that would take me to meet Sarah, a lady I had met online and had offered to house my travel bags while I went about in search of a house of my own, and obtain my British resident permit from the post office. I was clad in jeans and my favourite orange sweatshirt, which was supposed to be my defence against the cold wind, but on the contrary, it embraced the cold so that I could have sworn I was wearing a singlet. The cold blew through my sweatshirt and into me. I was literally naked to the icy wind. The only protection I had was the head warmer on my head.

'How do you people cope with this kind of cold?' I asked Sarah on a phone call.

'Did I not warn you?' she shot back, laughing. 'Hope you came prepared?'

I was about to answer when the wind came in full force, pushing me both ways as I strode down a slope. 'I will call you back,' I shouted into the phone as I struggled against the wind while trying to keep my bags still. Less than an hour later, I was at Sarah's. As I ate the fried rice she served me, I wished I had eaten earlier; perhaps the wind wouldn't have been able to toss me about.

At noon, I arrived at the post office for my BRP. The post-office clerk handed me a paper number and informed me I could wait for collection or return later. I chose to wait – where else had I to go? I moved to join the number of people by the corner also awaiting their BRPs when I tipped my head towards the rack of postcards, and I was at once consumed by the sight of a lady I swore was an angel, who possessed an air of splendour portrayed across her charming face oozing beauty and simplicity. She was clad in an orange-resembling shirt tucked into blue slim-fitting jeans with white sneakers; the cold air brushed mild against her skin because of the black winter jacket she had on. She flung her hair back and reached for her phone, while I stared mesmerised in self-conflict over her birth country. Embodied with sensual full petite lips on a slim face, moderate eyes and tapered cheekbones, I settled my gaze on her red polished nails and concluded she was Black British.

I moved up the queue to the front and met the post-office clerk. He took my card number, then my passport, and examined it for a few seconds.

'Just a moment,' he said, and left to get my document. I turned around, and there she was, behind me, touching her phone while it charged in a socket. I let out a smile at fate.

'Are you Nigerian or Ghanaian?' I asked with probing sincerity.

She looked up, and with a cheerful smile said, 'I am Nigerian.' There was humility in her voice, and a touch of purity in her expression. She was adorable.

'Really!? I swear you don't look it. I am Alex,' I offered her my hand.

'Fareeda,' she replied with a smile. She shook my hand. Though I could not feel the warmth of her skin because of the black glove shielding her hand, I felt it in her smile.

'What school are you in?'

'University of Glasgow,' she replied. 'You?'

I gasped. Fate had done more than I imagined. We talked about school registration and I made an attempt to help her with course enrolment. We exchanged numbers and said our goodbyes.

I had not imagined that I would see Fareeda anytime soon, but I saw her an hour after noon the next day at school in Fraser's building. I had always been one to believe there was no such thing as coincidence except it was coincidence, and this was no longer a coincidence.

'Hey! What's up?' she grinned.

'Hey. I'm good.' I sat beside her. 'How did your class go?'

I was waiting for my class which was to begin at 3 p.m., and it afforded us ample time to talk. She narrated how her lecturer had refused her entry into the class having missed two classes prior. We made a joke of it and talked about as many things we could in the couple of hours we spent together, yet it wasn't enough. I learnt a lot about her, more from the things she didn't say than the things she did, and every uncovering left me intrigued.

'I intend to arrive at class a few minutes late.'

'Why?' was her curious response.

'Kind of like an all eyes on me thing when I enter,' I lied.

I relished our hours together and needed an excuse to stay a few more. She oozed exuberance, but our conversations took my mind off worrying over where I would sleep at night. I was prepared for the worse – to sleep on the concourse of Buchanan bus station.

After class, on my way to nothingness at bus station, my phone beeped. It was a text from Adenike. It read:

You can come for house viewing tomorrow at 10am

Two days earlier, she had put up a shared apartment ad, and I indicated my interest to take the place. I informed her I was ready to move in straight away, but she refused and insisted she would inform me when she would be free for me to view the house. If only she knew.

I bumped my fist amidst shuddering in the incessant cold wind. I was, however, confident that by tomorrow, I would have a place to sleep. I only had the night to worry about sleeping out in the cold.

I got onto the bus. I was attempting to pay the bus fare when I heard my name from the back seat.

'Alex!'

I turned towards the voice, which sounded all too familiar. A woman was waving at me, smiling. I looked closer; it was Fareeda. I let out a relieved smile and paid the fare. She was just who I wanted to see before my long night. She was with a Chinese course-mate; we bumped fists and I sat behind her, my eyes on the road, but wide enough to steal glances at them. She introduced me to her course-mate, who then told me her name, but I heard nothing, I only knew it ended with 'ling'. I just nodded with a smile and said, 'Nice to meet you.'

At the bus station, Fareeda and I walked slowly to her bus-stand, laughing over how she had missed her stop the previous day and ended up getting home at almost midnight. When her bus arrived, she stood last in the queue, affording us a few more minutes together.

'I wonder how their pizza tastes here? It better be sweet like they make it look in their movies,' I said.

'The one I tried earlier was not bad,' she chuckled. 'You should try it too.'

'Oh trust me, there are a lot of things I want to try, like tacos for a start.'

'Really!? Me too,' she retorted and we both laughed. 'There's no need to rush anything. We will have enough time to try everything.'

We both nodded, then came a solemn silence. Those were the exact same words my old flame had said to me at the inception of our relationship, but with Fareeda, I knew it was different. I was dazed with an incredible fondness which filled me with warmth – and especially in a cold strange land – but not in a romantic or sexual way. I waved her goodbye and went into the concourse, full of travellers and passers-by moving into and out of town. I sat, heaving a mental sigh as I reflected over the long night ahead of me. '*All die na die*,' I told myself.

At the corner of the concourse was a Greggs store which sold snacks, and I thought to buy a pizza and a cup of tea as an excuse to sit in their store all night, away from the cold wind that whooshed into the concourse whenever the automatic doors slid open for people walking in. Besides, I was on an empty stomach since Sarah's. An hour later, a blonde lady with a broad grin, and clad in a Greggs store T-shirt, stood at the centre of the store.

'Hiya,' she twirled. 'Just wanted to let you all know that we'll be closing the store in a few minutes, thank you,' she announced still smiling, and returned to cleaning the floor.

'Shit!' I gulped down the tea I had been sipping for almost an hour, returned to the concourse, took my seat and watched them lock up the store. A few minutes later, someone with a head warmer and a backpack joined me. I gave him a nod.

'What's up. You're Nigerian?' he asked.

'Yes. And you?'

'Same.' We nodded and shook hands. 'Correct.' He looked at my backpack, leaned closer and in a low tone asked, '*How fa, shey na here you wan sleep this night?*'

'Brotherly, *na so we see am*, inside life,' I responded.

We laughed and shook hands again, this time alive and relieved probably from knowing that we would be swimming in the same waters.

'What's the name?' he asked.

'Alex. You?'

'Ernest.'

We shook hands again.

'Where did you sleep last night?' he asked.

'A friend helped me pay for an Airbnb. Two days now bro, you won't believe I've not taken my bath,' I laughed.

'Same with me,' said Ernest. 'I almost wanted to sleep at the bus station yesterday. Last minute, someone reached out and offered to accommodate me for one night.'

'Such is life. I heard getting an accommodation in Glasgow wasn't always this difficult.'

'It's not funny,' said Ernest, 'especially that our fellow Nigerians refuse to accommodate people stranded. But why are Nigerians here wicked? It is not like someone is asking to be accommodated permanently, just till one can secure an apartment. *Haba*! It is not fair.' He said it with an iota of disgust. 'The Indians are brothers to each other, that is why they thrive here.'

I thought about telling him about my experience of how Ben had pleaded with his friend, a Nigerian in Glasgow, to accommodate me for the night to avoid me sleeping in the open cold, but instead of helping, he sent me a text to give a flimsy excuse, then unoffered to help. Telling Ernest would spark a furious fire in him, so I didn't. I made a joke of it instead.

'One can't really blame them too,' he continued in the same breath, 'there are some people you help and it becomes trouble for you.' He sighed and shook his head. 'Regardless, it's not nice.'

'True.'

'I agree.'

We sat back in silence.

'There is this shared apartment I went to view today,' Ernest said. 'I pray I get it,' he said with a gesture of disdain.

'But?'

'I doubt I will get it.'

'Why?'

'The girl said she would have to pray about it first, that I am the third person who has come to view.'

'*Wahalla* for devil's children like us,' I said. He let out a silent hiss and we laughed.

'*Na church girl jare*,' he said in pidgin English. 'She won't want a flatmate like me.'

'Why?'

'My grey hair. She might see me as an old guy who would cause her stress.' In between my laughter, he added, 'Imagine I eventually get the place and she invites me to her church after stressing me like this. I will curse her.'

We laughed.

'I have viewing tomorrow too. The lady said I should come by ten a.m.'

'Lady! Are you sure it's not the same place?'

'I doubt. The place is located towards Paisley.'

'Same as the place I checked too.'

'Really!'

'Yeah. I have a feeling it is the same place. What is her name?'

'I am not sure. Our chat wasn't more than wanting the house.'

'Let me see her profile picture.'

I unlocked my phone and showed him. His face lit up.

'It is the same girl. Adenike.'

'Ah, yes, Adenike.' I paused for a few seconds and said, '*Wahalla*. I have entered one chance.' We laughed. 'After tomorrow, she will include me in her prayers for a perfect flatmate too,' we laughed again, this time harder.

'She might fancy you. Young and fresh, unlike me, old and grey.' He rubbed his grey hair and frowned. 'This grey hair has done me more harm than good. No one believes I am young.'

We laughed. I checked the time on my phone; it was 10:45.

'I know what to do.' I slid my phone back into my pocket and looked up at Ernest. 'As she is a church girl, I will give her church boy vibes. In fact, when she sees me, she will see Jesus in me.' I laughed, Ernest almost choked on his laughter. Our laughter came to a sudden stop when a male voice, from the speakers above the ceiling, echoed over the concourse.

'Attention, attention. The concourse will be closing at eleven. Please complete your activities. Thank you.'

I froze, sunk over the realisation that the only place left for shelter was the open waiting area of the bus station. I turned to Ernest, who had the same look.

'I thought this place is open twenty-four hours,' Ernest's voice quaked.

'My guess is, the concourse closes, but the bus station is open for twenty-four hours.'

I was mentally stimulating my brain in advance against the next few hours I would be open to the naked cold. I spun to the waiting area and watched as people shivered while they sat waiting for their buses. I turned back to Ernest.

'There's no going back now. *All die na die.*' I hurled a hefty sigh.

He nodded. We sat in silence, and started for the waiting area only when the guards began locking the doors. When the door we walked through slid open, the cold wind which greeted us went through my shirt and sent shivers to my skin. I knew it was going to be a long cold night, but was confident I would survive. I managed to take out my phone to check the temperature, it was five degrees but felt like one degree. I swallowed no longer confident of surviving, as only my head was protected from the cold.

'Guy!' Ernest exclaimed, shivering at the edge of the coloured metal chair he sat on. 'Even with my winter jacket, I am shaking.' His eyes widened as if he was seeing me for the first time. 'See what you are wearing!?'

'What to do?' I smiled. 'I will survive.'

'Ha! You are strong. I can't even try what you're trying.'

I tried to laugh, but halfway through, I felt my teeth tremble. I closed my mouth and nodded with a grin instead.

'See, we will not try this again,' said Ernest with a sense of candour. 'I won't wish this on my enemy.'

'Never,' I said. I looked about me and with certainty reiterated, 'Never!'

The night grew mature and icier, but the clock moved at an unhurried pace. Maybe it was because I kept staring – through the transparent doors – at the big wall clock in the concourse, or because nature took delight in watching me shiver after I had boasted to Sarah that my sweatshirt was stronger than any cold weather. If only nature knew I was foolish and mistook Nigeria's cold weather for Glasgow's.

Ernest positioned his bag against the chair, leaned on it and closed his eyes to sleep. He opened them a few seconds later, gave me a serious look, shook his head and returned to sleep. I could tell it was look of pity, in case he woke and I had frozen to death.

I stood all through the night with my hands tucked in my pockets. Some moments were busy; I watched buses bringing in and taking out travellers. Other moments were cold. Horribly cold.

A few minutes before 6 a.m., Ernest woke up. He said nothing, but I was sure he was surprised I was still standing. The concourse opened. We raced in. I went to Greggs store, bought two cups of tea and sausages which I couldn't pronounce, but I didn't care, I needed the warmth from the tea, so did Ernest. We sat on a chair close to the toilet entrance. Before eating, we took turns to sneak into the toilet to brush our teeth, then afterwards settled upon the hot tea and unknown sausage lying before us.

Ernest left for his school. I left to view the house.

'Good afternoon,' I greeted Adenike on entering the apartment.

'I just came back from work and am feeling very sleepy, but I promised, so here we are.'

'Thank you,' I said with a silent cheer.

I took off my head warmer like a gentleman and stepped into the passage. The passage was warm. I felt warmth. She knocked on the door to the room which I would occupy if I got the place. The door opened. The occupant was busy arranging his clothes into his bag. He gave me a nod and I nodded back. The tour ended after viewing the bathroom, it was tidy and clean. The whole apartment was.

'I love this,' I turned to her and said. 'I want to take it already. To tell you the truth, before I stepped into the building, I whispered to God and said if this place is mine, he should give it to me.'

She let out a grin.

For the first time, using the word truth in a lie fused with God's name, it didn't sound like a crime, it sounded like the truth.

'The room won't be available until Sunday,' she said, 'and you're not the only one who has come to view this place.'

'Oh, okay,' I nodded.

'We want somebody who won't be trouble...' she was saying

'You have found me,' I cut in cheerfully.

'And the landlord has some of his stuffs in one part of the

wardrobe, it's why we want a guy, because they don't have tons of load.'

'That's no problem.' I retorted. 'I don't have stuffs. In fact, one Nigerian girl saw I travelled with just two bags and was vexed at me. I am sure she would have beaten me if she had the chance.' I laughed and Adenike grinned. She was lethargic and hence inscrutable; I couldn't exactly tell if I was making an impression on her.

'Move in date is on the Sunday. I will have to think over it before picking the next occupant, and speak to my brother too. He rented it before I moved in.'

I nodded, and wondered why she didn't say she would pray about it. I was prepared to give a sermon to chockfull her ears.

'No problem,' I said with a broad smile. 'I know the Holy Spirit will lead you accordingly.' She grinned. I kept on the momentum. 'This place is the only place I have viewed,' I said as she walked me to the door, 'and I really do like it. I mean, I know I shouldn't say this so it doesn't influence your choice, but I slept at the bus station yesterday night.' I noticed a hint of compassion sweep across her face and I was pleased. 'Don't feel sad, it was nothing,' I said with triviality. 'I just know God is with me, even in this place.' She gave a light chuckle. For the first time I studied her face, her beauty was apparent; the picture on her WhatsApp status didn't tell the whole truth.

'So where will you stay now?' she asked.

'I am going to Colchester to stay with my friend hoping by next week Monday before my next class, I would have sorted my accommodation.'

'Okay.'

'Thank you,' I let out one last smile before taking the lift down into the cold.

That weekend in Colchester, on my way to the club to dance away my worries, my phone rang. The caller introduced himself as Adenike's brother.

'My sister told me about you. She is really compassionate about what you've gone through,' he said.

I smiled. I had conquered.

'We don't want someone who is disorganised and will cause trouble,' he continued. 'I hope that won't be you?'

'You don't have to worry about that,' I said with conviction. 'I am as organised as far as organisation is concerned.'

'The rent is paid every first day of a new month. If you're willing to take the place...

'Willing!?' I cut him short. 'I am taking the place.'

'Okay great,' he said. 'Some of the rules are...'

I moved farther away from the road to hear him clearly as the sound of speeding vehicles kept impeding my hearing. Even so, I barely heard a thing he said, but I said 'Okay,' at the end of his every sentence. 'So we look forward to having you with us,' he concluded.

'Thank you,' I said, 'and please thank Adenike for me.'

The call ended just in time for the bus to arrive. I texted Fareeda. She was as excited as I was. I got to the club. I partied harder than the previous night.

I arrived in Glasgow Monday morning and found my way to school. After class, I went to Sarah's to get my belongings before heading to my new place. I knocked on the door and Adenike opened it. She wore on her face a compassionate look and a warm smile which melted the cold lingering over me.

'How was your day?' she asked with a tranquil voice.

I shook my head and heaved a deep sigh of relief. 'It was fucked. I took the wrong bus. I had to trek from where I stopped down to this place. It wasn't funny.'

'Sorry,' she said in a soothing and tranquil manner. 'You are welcome, just go in and rest.'

'Thank you.'

I slept that night without caring to unpack.

I spent the next three days going to school and returning back home. I ate and drank nothing. I had opened a bank account with a few pounds in it, but had no ATM card to withdraw money, neither did I have cash. I knew no one to ask for assistance, so I decided to wait for Friday when my card would arrive. Friday came, the card didn't arrive and I knew I must either find a way to eat or I would die from hunger and not cold.

That Friday evening, on my way home, knowing *all die na die*, I walked into the Sainsbury's store beside Buchanan bus station. I looked around for any security officer to approach. There was one wearing a yellow reflective jacket. I set out towards him.

'Good evening sir,' I greeted the man. He had a bald head and was Black, but he was not Nigerian. 'Please, I need your help.'

The man gave an acknowledging nod and I continued. 'I opened an online bank and applied for a bank card but won't get it until Monday or Tuesday. I do not have any cash on me and have not eaten in three days. I want to transfer money to you so you can help me withdraw it.'

The man chuckled, then let out what I later realised was a smile while shaking his head with reluctance.

'No, no, no,' he lamented. 'I can't do that. A lot of things can go wrong. You are Nigerian, and I know what some of you do here. You get my account details and in minutes all my money is gone.'

I was dumbstruck. Defeated. Stung by the injurious stigma of being Nigerian. Put out by the reality of another hungry day.

'I understand you,' the man continued, 'but I have to be careful too. I am Gambian.'

I nodded. I didn't even know why. I just did.

He flashed me a sorry gaze, looked down to my stomach and back to my face. 'You said you are hungry, pick anything, but not more than five pounds.' He pointed towards the shelves.

I hesitated with uncertainty, wondering if he meant he would pay for whatever I picked. I didn't want to ask what he meant so as not to sound worrying, but I knew if I didn't ask and went on to pick items and he refused to pay, I would be branded a thief and declared guilty without trial. Thanks to the colour of my skin.

'Sorry,' I said, putting on a serious visage, 'do you mean I should pick anything worth five pounds and you would pay?'

'Yes,' he nodded. 'You said you're hungry, right?'

I nodded with vigour and hurried to grab a loaf of bread, bottle of water, a tin of sardines and a can of tomato paste – even though I wasn't sure why I needed tomato paste. A part of me just wanted to pick items that totalled five pounds. I went to the man and he directed me to the self-service machine. He showed me how to operate it and paid. I thanked him. At the door on my way out, I thanked him again.

When I got home that night, I sat on the rug in my room and

spread my legs wide open. I ate my fill, and when I couldn't move my body, I lay flat on my back and slept.

The next morning, on a Saturday, for the first time since I moved in, I went around the house and met Adenike in the kitchen.

'Good morning,' I greeted her on opening the door. She swivelled and jerked, placing her hand over her chest. 'Were you scared?' I asked on watching her break into a chuckle.

'Yes. I am used to being alone. My previous flatmate was almost never home.'

I chuckled. 'Not anymore,' I teased. She returned to her cooking.

'What bank do you use? I want to open a standard bank account so I can get a card on time.'

'Bank of Scotland,' she said. 'It's easy. You can do it online.'

'Okay, thanks.'

'So how are you enjoying Glasgow?' she asked cheerfully.

'Everything is fine except the weather. It is bloody cold.'

She chuckled. 'You will get used to it,' she assured, stirring the Jollof rice in the pot. 'By the way, I added rice for you.'

'Thank you,' I grinned. Through the corner of my eyes, I stole a glance at the pot of rice. The food looked impressive.

'I have been wanting to ask,' said Adenike. 'How have you been eating? You leave early and come back at night, and I don't want to disturb you.'

It was the manner in which she asked, the hint of concern in her voice, and the serene aura in her gesticulation which compelled me to tell her of my experience. She stared at me with her mouth opened in awe. Her eyes had the same expression as when I told her about sleeping in the bus station.

'You should have asked me,' she responded with a fusion of anger and empathy; the tone of her voice caressed my pain.

'I didn't want to disturb you,' I said with modesty.

'Well, I understand you because I could be like that too. One thing I've learnt in this place is that you should ask for help when you need it.'

'I've learnt my lesson now,' I laughed.

I leaned against the table in the kitchen as we talked, moving from one topic to the other. It was the second time I noticed her beauty. There was something different about the way it unravelled, imprinting itself in your memory, along with a beam which generously shines at will. Everything about her was meek, down to the way she walked.

The third time I noticed the difference in her beauty was when her white male friend visited. I was heading to the kitchen to drink water, I opened the door to the sitting room, and there she was, sitting leaned against the wall in her usual cheerful manner. I smiled at her and gave her a nod. She smiled back.

'Meet my friend, Roland,' I think she said. I didn't quite catch his name but we shook hands anyway. 'My flatmate, Alex,' she told him. He was eating Jollof rice. He was the one she had mentioned loved Nigerian rice and asked for it whenever he came visiting. We joked over how the whites would eat our food if given the chance. The only thing they wouldn't be able to take was peppery food, especially the Yoruba kind of pepper.

'Was that...' Roland mentioned the name of a popular British rock band, 'you were playing?' I couldn't comprehend the name he said, not with rice dangling in his mouth combined with his naturally twisted tongue.

'Yeah,' I nodded, but I had no idea what he said. The songs playing from my phone were from Nation Radio Scotland; I had grown fond of them. 'Do you like music?' I asked him.

He paused to mull for a moment and I wondered how hard it could be to like or not to like music.

'Pretty much,' he nodded, seemingly half convinced. 'Except for Taylor Swift.'

'Oh!' I gasped. 'For real?' He nodded. 'You don't know what you're missing. You should listen to her 1989 album.'

'I don't know,' he winced. 'I will give it a try.'

'You should.'

'I think I am beginning to like Burna Boy though,' he said with delight. 'Adenike has been playing me his songs.'

'They call me Burnaaaa Boy,' I sang it in the manner Burna Boy used to.

Adenike smiled and said, 'That is a true fan.' I nodded with smugness noting we both loved the same artist.

'Nice meeting you,' I said to Roland.

'Some other time, yeah,' he offered his hand and we shook. I went to drink my water, all along wondering how one person could be beauty personified with three shades of beauty. I checked the meaning of her name. It meant to be deserving of her beauty. She was.

'Is she single?' Ben had asked me over the phone the first time I told him my flatmate was a female.

'Yes,' I think so.

'Then everything is settled. You're single, she is single. Just start to plan marriage.'

I laughed.

'It is not funny, my man,' Ben continued. 'Single plus single equals married.'

'I am not thinking of marriage now; neither am I looking for love,' I told him.

'Then what are you looking for?' he asked with contempt.

I tilted my head to the corner to stare at my window hoping it'd reflect an answer, but it only reflected the bookish wallpaper across the walls of my room.

'I don't know,' I replied. 'Not like I'd run away from love if it comes, but I am not actively searching. If you know what I mean.'

Ben hissed. 'Mumu.'

When I told Phoebe during one of our chats, I was convinced if it had occurred over a phone call, I would have felt the contempt in her voice too.

'Wait! Your flatmate is a she?' Phoebe texted. 'I should begin preparing my wedding outfits.'

I was still laughing at the message when another one delivered.

'Because are you thinking what I am thinking?'

'No,' I wrote back, laughing. 'I am not thinking what I think you are thinking.'

As days went by, the zephyr wind that blew cold soon whooshed away, and with it the euphoria of moving into a new country, giving way for blustery winds to terrorise the air, yet, with such ghastly wind came a certain kind of lonesomeness that permeated the air above me. I sat on my bed, visited by pangs of solitude. It dawned on me that I was a stranger in a far-flung land unable to visit home at whim, family and friends pined apart across mountains and seas, and the only thing that felt close to home were WhatsApp calls.

'Somehow, I feel alone yet anew,' I texted Fareeda.

'Why?' she wrote back, '*wassup*?'

'I don't even know. I guess I am overwhelmed with the feeling of being in a new place and attempting to build my career from scratch. I mean, I've always been far from home, but this is a different kind of far.'

'Don't feel like that,' came her reply, but I could hear her speak. 'If you feel like that, how would I feel?'

I laughed and wrote back, 'Strong man like me is already feeling a way he doesn't know. It seems I am no longer liking this country.'

She sent a laughing emoji and a meme. She often spoke more with memes than words.

'I am fine,' I told her. 'It's just a moment of doubt. Nothing more.' It became clear to me what Ben meant when he always said, 'If care is not taken, one can easily get depressed in this country.'

The feeling of solitude that night cast a different kind of cold behind the shut windows. The heater in my room wasn't working, which made it worse. When night fell, I didn't want to spend it alone, unwilling to sleep in doubt and wake up the same way. Everything everywhere all at once was unfolding around me. I was unsure what was real and what wasn't, fighting to stay awake beneath my duvet. I held my phone tight, trying to type with shivering fingers as the cold diddled with my head.

'When did the landlord say he is coming to fix the heater in my room? I can't continue like this,' I texted Adenike.

'He said tomorrow. Why? Are you okay?' she texted back.

'I think I am shivering to my death,' I replied with a lie that could as well pass as the truth.

'Can I come to your room? Just for tonight.' I paused and waited for her reply. When there was none, I added, 'So I don't freeze to death.' I added the freezing emoji.

I once looked into her room while walking through the passage as her room door was flung open. Her room was bigger than mine, her bed too. Mine was a single foam resting upon a terribly made wood frame dressed in white and blue stripes, hers was a double bed adorned with pink. *Pink!* I had winced.

She didn't reply, nor was there any indication of her typing a response. I wondered if I had been too brazen, and if to delete the message, but it was too late, she had read it. If she frowned at my message, I would simply claim I had mistyped with dizzy knocked-out eyes. Yet, despite my moral dilemma not to be presumptuous, I refused to endure the icy lone night.

'*lol*,' she replied.

I waited for a few seconds but there was no indication that she was typing. I watched the phone closely as if my life depended on it.

'You can come,' she typed back. 'It won't be nice to wake tomorrow and find my flatmate frozen.' She added a laughing emoji.

I heard her unlock the door to her room. The smile on my face was reflected on my phone's screen.

Her room was warm and dark, only lit by the bed lamp at the corner of her bed, however enough to reveal her blue transparent nightgown.

'Make yourself comfortable,' she said, and pointed to the bed. 'Don't be shy.'

I forced a grin and nodded, befuddled how she read through me. I took off my sweatshirt and joined her beneath the duvet.

'Are you still feeling cold?' she asked.

'Not even if the windows were open.'

Adenike grinned. Her face was half lit from the bed lamp and I could barely see her features, but I was accustomed to the shape of her mouth when she smiled.

'Your bed is big. Doesn't it feel lonely sleeping alone?'

'Since my brother left, I have gotten used to being alone. So no, it doesn't.'

I grinned at the buoyancy in her voice, the woven tendrils on her head and the stillness of her lips.

'Goodnight,' she said breaking the silence.

'I want to kiss you,' I retorted.

She paused and stared me in ambivalence. I could tell she was taken aback by my audacity. She inhaled, exhaled, then closed her eyes, and I took the moment to kiss her. Her lips were obliging when our lips met, pliant, receptive and comely. I pulled back and cast a long gaze at her. Her silence was golden, but I heard her loud and clear, she didn't want to endure another night alone. I took off her nightgown and we made raw, urgent, intricate love all night.

I woke at the break of dawn on the same side of the bed I had slept. Then I was on my bed, in my room staring at the walls and not Adenike. For the first time since I had arrived, I felt alive, undaunted and poised about the new world I was in. I took out my laptop and began to write about last night, but my memory was hazy, too dark to recall her visage as she wriggled beneath me, nor how long into the night we lasted. But I did remember moving my fingers down her chest through every edge of the curve of her lips and its sweet nectar taste.

A few pages into writing my experience last night, I went to the sitting room to continue writing and met Adenike tidying the kitchen.

'Hey. Good morning.'

'Good morning,' she turned around with a smile. 'You look really excited.'

'Yeah. I had the best night of my life,' I said.

'Really!? What happened?'

I opened my mouth to speak then paused. 'It's nothing to worry about,' I said.

I grabbed a chair from the dining room and joined her in the kitchen.

'I see you're writing. Found the inspiration you were looking for?'

'Very much so.'

'That is great,' she replied.

'You can say that again.'

'Nice. I am making toasted bread, care for some?'

'Sure. Thanks.'

I had spent a few minutes writing when my phone rang. I reluctantly reached to pick up.

'Hello.'

'Heya! Molly here from Konstellation, am I on to Alex?' came the female voice from the other end of the phone.

Is it me, or is it that every Scottish woman is called Molly? I winced. 'Yes, Alex here.'

'Great. We received your application and wanted to ask a few follow-up questions. Do you have your documents with you at the moment?'

'No, just hold on a few seconds.' I dashed to my room.

The call lasted about five minutes, then I headed back to the kitchen. I met Adenike sitting beside my laptop with a frown on her face. I froze and began to pray her eyes didn't wander to what I had written.

'I thought you said you don't lie,' Adenike turned to me.

'I don't. At least I try not to,' I replied, downcast, knowing where this was headed.

'Then why did you lie about last night?' she spun the laptop to face me.

I swallowed.

She slammed her fist on the table and stood to me. 'Alex. I need you to start talking.'

'I can explain.' I opened my mouth but the words didn't come out, nothing in my mind I thought I could say made sense. 'I was in doubt about everything, and the thought of us making love kept me going through the night,' I said, hoping it made enough sense.

She popped open her eyes dumbstruck. It was obvious she was convinced that I was foolish. I too was convinced I was.

She shook her head and went to switch off the toasting machine, handed me my bread on a plate, and as I made to collect it, she threw it into the waste bin and started for her room.

'Adenike, please.'

'Please what?' she retorted.

'Fine. I admit that I find you attractive, that I have imagined grabbing you from behind and whispering into your ear while you cook, and how it'd feel like kissing you. But no, never have I thought about having sex with you.'

'Until last night,' she shot back.

'I was cold and in doubt.'

She looked at me in dismay, shook her head and went into her room, slamming the door hard against any attempt to approach.

I heaved a sigh and cursed beneath my breath.

Five days passed and I barely saw Adenike, and the few times I did, she strode past like I didn't exist. It wasn't the first time we would go a day without seeing or speaking to each other, but this was the first time her silence was golden. The silence was emotionless.

One windy afternoon at the tail end of autumn, the doorbell rang and I picked up the phone receiver.

'Hello. Who is there?' I spoke into the phone.

There was no response, just the familiar sound of a person breathing at the other end of the bell. I pressed the entrance button, hung the phone up and went to open the front door.

'Welcome,' I greeted Adenike, but she walked straight past me. I ran ahead to prevent her from entering her room. 'Adenike please, talk to me. Your silence is killing me.'

She stepped back and stared at me from head to toe with a scornful gaze. 'You are not dying enough,' she said with a cruel sombre tone and brushed past my hand into her room.

I sat on the floor of the passage opposite her room, deserving of her anger but determined for her forgiveness. I soon began to shiver.

'Adenike,' my voice quaked. 'I won't leave till you talk to me. I don't care if I die from the cold.'

That would be foolishness, warned an inner voice, to which I agreed. But at least, I wanted her to believe I would. A minute later, the door to her room swung open and she walked past to the kitchen without batting an eye at me. I thought to attempt preventing her from entering her room but didn't. She returned to her door and stood by the side scrutinising me with her full blue eyes. She gestured I enter and I hurried after her from fear she might change her mind. She sat on the bed and I joined her, careful not to sit too close beside her, using the moments of silence to embrace the warmth from the heater.

'What is it you want from me?' she asked.

'Your forgiveness.'

'For what?' she scowled, 'Your imagination!? Please!'

'Then why are you angry at me?' I asked, bemused.

'I am not. I was just upset.'

'Upset about?' I wanted to ask. *What if I had sat out there in the cold, hoping for your forgiveness and died in that hope. I would have died for nothing!?* I thought. *Women*! I gritted my teeth in silence.

'How long have you been writing?' she asked with less tension in the tone of her voice.

'A couple of years. Why?'

'I like the way you weaved your words. I almost believed that night happened.'

I let out a smug grin but quickly took it back when she flashed me a frown.

'Thank you,' I said with modesty. 'I am glad you liked it. I mean like my writing.'

She lay back and stared at me in amusement. I chuckled. 'What?'

'So you imagine kissing and making love to me? What an imagination you have.'

'Oh no, please don't go there. You're making me shy.'

'Shy- shy bobo,' she teased.

We laughed harder, and our laughter died at the same time.

'So do you?'

'Do I what?' I asked.

'Want to kiss me and taste my nectar sip,' she grinned, coyly fixing her hair behind her ears.

I searched her eyes; they were plain and devoid of trickery. We blushed in silence then she leaned forward and closed her eyes. I leaned in and paused halfway still in doubt, but she didn't flinch and I didn't hold back. Her lips were more than I had imagined, full and rounded, the velvety of paradise, tasting of Prunus japonica. This time, the night was long. It was a night we would live to remember.

THE DEVIL HAS A SOUL

Are you a witch?
Are you
Have you had relations with
the devil?
Have you
Have you had relations with
the devil and what took place?

                                      Rebecca Tamas: Witch

Omonigho frowned and murmured almost every five minutes on the drive to the court house. It was a bumpy ride which made him uncomfortable, but most especially, he was in no hurry to be driven to his judgement. At some point, he thought he would again and again hit the body of the Black Maria van and yell at the driver to stop speeding and driving into potholes for fun, but such an action he knew would attract its consequences. He decided to bear the pain as today would be his last ride in the van. He managed to squeeze himself into a corner but it didn't stop him from jumping and swaying aimlessly. He hit his head on the ceiling of the rusty aluminium van again and he let out a low squawk, his head not yet accustomed to the pain. The officers must have heard him moan, because they cackled mockingly at him.

They arrived early at the Ikeja magistrate court and already the place was replete with a vicious crowd that kept throwing crumpled papers and empty plastic bottles at him. He felt good within himself as he evaded the objects thrown at him, and not even the shouts and screams could make him feel bad.

'Kill him, he is guilty.'

'…he deserves jungle justice and not the court…'

'Curse the day you were born.'

'…yes, burn him alive…'

'He is a wizard.'

'He is the devil.'

Omonigho ignored their anger, they were after all emotional and consciously ignoring the fact that he too was a victim. The majority of the thrown items were hitting the policemen that escorted him as it was their duty to guard and protect him. Omonigho laughed at the irony of a criminal being protected by the same people that had caught him.

'Throw him in the dock,' one officer commanded as they entered the court and Omonigho chuckled, having heard those exact words repeatedly at the same time and almost at the exact spot that one would think the officer practised it before every court hearing.

'Did I say something funny?' the officer asked with a frown. Omonigho shook his head.

'I would have ordered my men to strip and beat you, but today is your judgement so I'll let the judge do the beating,' said the officer with a smirk, then walked away. Omonigho was thrown into the dock and his cuffs removed.

The judge, then the twelve-man jury arrived, and as usual, their presence was honoured. The judge, whom Omonigho thought was difficult to portray for his lack of bodily shape, settled his spectacles on his nose, swivelled, struck the gavel against the sound block and there was order. The sound of the gavel could be likened to a furious thunder at the dawn of rapture, and this was his rapture. *The authority in wood*, Omonigho thought. The proceedings began. The judge asked the prosecution and the defence to make their final cases, as if anything said would change his mind or that of the jury who stared at Omonigho with condemnation.

'Omonigho,' the judge called after both lawyers had rounded up their cases, 'you have the right to address the court at this point. Do you have any final words?'

Omonigho thought for a moment about what he would say, and how he would say it, and the only thing that came to his head was, *as she was a woman I loved her, as she was a witch, she paid the price for stealing my destiny and denying me the future I dreamed of.* Omonigho turned to his lawyer and saw him glaring at him. The lawyer didn't exactly know what he was thinking, but knowing Omonigho, he knew whatever it was he was thinking would show no empathy and could ruin their chances of being acquitted or at least getting a sentence other than a whole life order or worse, as that was what he faced for murdering a woman in cold blood.

'No my lord,' said Omonigho to the judge.

'Over to you,' announced the judge to the jurors.

The foreperson of the jury stood and read to the court their deductions, coming to the conclusion that Omonigho's actions were premeditated and consciously executed, and carefully precluding the defendant's plea of mental instability which Omonigho's lawyer claimed was as a result of the many ill deeds of the late Glory Edewor to his client, which in turn led to his inhumane action and therefore to him being not guilty of first-degree murder. Everything the juror said sounded confusing in Omonigho's ear. This was the third time in two months they were convening in court over what he felt should have been judged on the first day of the hearing. The lawyers and the judge prolonged the case with their elaborate words, which had made him believe his lawyer's promise that if he did as he said, he would have a get out of jail free card, but from the look on their faces, it seemed to him those promises were just words.

'Tomorrow, in court,' Omonigho's lawyer had said to him, 'I'll make a motion to withdraw our plea of not guilty and enter a plea of guilty. You just have to do what I say. If all things go as expected, you could have your life back.'

'How?' Omonigho asked, confused.

The lawyer began to explain, and even though Omonigho didn't understand word for word what his lawyer was saying, he comprehended he meant they would be moving from pleading not guilty and insane to guilty and insane. He was insane either way.

'If that works,' said Omonigho, 'then the law is really an ass.'

'Keep such attitude away from the court. It is repellent. What I am giving you is hope.'

'I heard hope is a dangerous thing,' retorted Omonigho.

'But it is all we have. All you have.'

The judged cleared his throat, bringing Omonigho out of his reminiscing, and rebalanced his glasses drifting off his nose. Omonigho grinned in anticipation of everything that the judge could possibly say. He had long expected and prepared for this moment, resolute that whatever was said – either it went his way or not – would not make him weep, and he would do his best not to look in the direction of his family.

'I have carefully examined this case,' began the judge, 'and there is only one question that I can't stop asking myself. Why? Omonigho Ogbamremu. Why did you decide to throw away your bright future?'

Omonigho thought the judge pronounced his name with little or no difficulty for a Yoruba man.

'You are such a bright man with a promising future. Why throw it all away over some claim which cannot be justified?'

For the first time since the crime, Omonigho wondered what would become of his life. Where his goals and aspirations would dwell, who would become the king he had hoped to be and build the kingdom he had dreamt of. The future flashed before his thin pale eyes and he immediately hated what he saw. It was a flash of an image of him surrounded by spikes, covered in tears and blood. He cursed himself and fate too, for directing Glory Edewor into his path. Their meeting had looked divine, but was doomed from the start, having more woes than Romeo and Juliet. He should have known not to trust his heart but his head, he should have reminded himself that love was the biggest scam in the world which crashes and burns, but he was too deep in love to listen to his head, howbeit when a man falls in love a new Mumu is born.

Listening to the judge speak, he wished he had taken the opportunity to tell the court the full story and not the pieces they had come to know through questions and answers. He wished he could tell the court that he was a victim too, that even though she was the most beautiful woman he had ever met and loved, she was a witch and he was her prey. He remembered it all; the first day he met her, it was during a Sunday service when the assistant pastor ended the bible reading and announced the welcoming of the choir as they took to the stage. None but one stole his gaze as he stared at her from the back seat where he sat with bliss in his eyes, wondering why until that day he hadn't taken notice of a divine beautiful being.

At the close of service, he went about greeting church members and making small conversations here and there to pass time while he waited patiently as the choristers did their monthly choir meeting. He met her at the door on her way out and introduced himself as Omonigho and told her how he had never seen her until that day. She told him she just got transferred to their parish a few weeks back and perhaps he hadn't been in church in the weeks she had been. He made a joke over his absence and they laughed as he walked her home. He loved everything about her, her smile, her voice, her serenity, and when he shook her hand, he could have sworn God was a woman. It was love at first sight for Omonigho, but she confessed she had seen him once during a zonal service and liked him; it was why she had asked to be transferred to his parish.

Glory Edewor soon became an assistant youth leader, fervent in church and in her love for Omonigho; their relationship was an open secret, they were a match made in heaven. Omonigho's meeting with Glory was ill-timed and at a dagger point, because he was still trying to figure out the direction of his life. He claimed to have finished his undergraduate programme but three years after he still had no certificate to prove it. He was a creative brimming with ideas which always began with enthusiasm but withered faster than autumn leaves, like when he was a practising DJ in his prime, yet, without any reason brought to an end a budding career. He was, however, always confident about one thing, which was that he would be a king, a ruler of nations, and this confidence he had always had from a tender age having been told so by a prophetess to whom his parents had taken him to consult about his future.

'I really love her,' Omonigho said to his closest friend, Etim Ekpo. 'I just want to marry her and live happy ever after.'

Etim laughed. 'Lover boy,' he said without giving it a thought, knowing Omonigho was merely enjoying his moments with her as he had with other girls. 'So what are you waiting for?'

'Money. I need to take my yahoo-yahoo seriously now. Any money I hit this period, straight to altar.' Omonigho replied with a grin on his face.

Etim chuckled and said nothing, even though with previous

girls, his friend had never been so in love to speak about marrying any. He also assumed his friend was wise enough to know he could not depend on fraudulent money to start and keep a family. Etim chuckled again, this time out loud and said, 'You are really funny, Omonigho. But I understand,' he said, scratching his beard, 'when a man falls in love, a new Mumu is born.'

They both laughed.

Omonigho leaned his back against the wall and stared into space for a few minutes, and then he brought his gaze back down and said smiling, 'We are just too perfect for each other. We are compatible.'

'Wait! Are you really in love? Like real love?'

Omonigho continued to speak without giving attention to Etim's question. 'She understands everything about me, especially when it relates to money. She barely asks me of it, and when she does and I don't have any to give, she never complains but tells me she understands.' He turned to Etim with a grin. 'Such women are hard to find these days.'

'And is that a good or bad thing?' asked Etim.

Omonigho flashed him a stern gaze and said, 'When people with girlfriend are talking, you keep quiet.'

Etim chuckled and said in a mocking tone, 'I go love o!'

The more the days went by, the more Omonigho was consumed with his love for Glory, often boasting of her faithfulness and that no other man could woo her and succeed. Then when he discovered she had been having sexual affairs with three other financially able men, he was heartbroken but quickly forgave her as the money she took from them benefited him too. Their relationship continued to blossom, not without its own troubles as common with all relationships, until the day Omonigho sent for Etim, and when Etim arrived, he greeted him by saying, 'I want to break up with Glory.'

Etim, who was about to swallow a spoon of vegetable rice, paused in awe then suddenly burst out laughing, but Omonigho didn't laugh. 'You are serious!?' exclaimed Etim. 'But why!?'

Omonigho inhaled and wiped his face, he mulled things over for a few seconds then looked around the house, but there was no one within hearing distance.

'A prophetess stopped my mum on the road to tell her that she has a son who is in danger, which is me.'

'Okay.'

'She said the girl I am sleeping with is a witch and I should break up with her.'

Etim wanted to laugh but instead held his breath for a few long seconds, not wishing to be insensitive. 'Wow!' he said instead. 'How did the prophetess know it was you?'

'She didn't, but when Mumsy narrated it to us, we knew it was me.'

'Wow!' Etim exclaimed again.

'How can Glory do this to me!?' asked Omonigho in an angry frustrated tone. 'After all I have done for her, a witch! Ha! This life is wicked.'

'Don't you think you should give her the benefit of the doubt? I mean, you don't know if this prophet—'

'Prophetess,' Omonigho corrected.

'If this prophetess is real or fake. There are—

'Prophetesses don't lie,' retorted Omonigho, 'it is prophets that do.'

Etim nodded at his deduction. 'If you say so.'

'This thing I want to tell you,' said Omonigho, 'I haven't told anybody, not even my mother.'

'Okay.'

'Maria, my ex, once told me that she saw Glory in a dream sleeping with her leg over my body.'

'She was pressing your Glory!?'

'Exactly. She was taking mine to fill hers.'

'Wow,' Etim exclaimed again, this time looking more confused than surprised.

'I think she must have blinded my eyes,' Omonigho said nodding. 'There are things I did I wouldn't have done.'

'Like?'

'I don't like short girls and she is short. I don't date fair girls, but she is fair. Now that I remember, I was also warned to be careful of fair women, as one would be the one to steal my crown. I think Glory is the girl that woman spoke of many years ago.'

Etim shook his head. 'I can't believe what I am hearing.'

'That was me at first, but I have confirmed and they all say the same thing, that she is a senior witch and is the reason I am not progressing.'

'Who is they?'

'I consulted with two Babalawos.'

Etim let out a soft sigh. He had almost forgotten his friend was a dangerous cultist and shrines were nothing scary to him.

'I am going to confront her,' said Omonigho after a minute of pondering and staring at pictures of them on his phone. 'I would ask her why me? Why couldn't she be the witch to make me prosperous rather than take what I already have?' he heaved a sigh and said again, 'I must confront her.'

'If she is as powerful as they say she is, then doing that would be you throwing caution to the wind. My guess is she already knows you know. Best is to slowly find a way to instigate a break-up without pricking her witchery pride.'

'Hmm! You speak wisdom.'

Being the witch that she was and probably knowing of his plan to break up with her, Glory made the possibility of the separation easy when she informed him that her sister in Abuja had given birth and she would be travelling to spend a little time with her. She had barely spent a week in Abuja when Omonigho broke up with her and went on to accuse her of stealing his glory. She cried. He cried too.

'It is for the best,' Etim told him. 'Now you just have to avoid her as much as possible.'

Omonigho avoided her for as much as four days when she returned to Lagos. He took her to a spiritual native doctor to cast away her witchery nature, it was a success and they went back to loving each other.

Two years later when Omonigho called Etim and began to cry, it was too difficult for Etim to understand because he had not seen his friend cry before.

'I am dead,' said Omonigho.

'You don't look dead,' replied Etim staring at him from head to toe.

'I defended her, fought for her, gave her a good name and reputation to live up to, yet, she could do all these things to me?'

'Who are you talking about?' asked Etim.

'Glory, who else,' barked Omonigho. 'She is still a witch and is still taking my glory. That is why my life has gone worse, can't you see it?'

Etim sat upright with the same shock he had on his face two years ago when he first heard these accusations. 'And you know this how?'

'There is this prophetess I was introduced to because I needed answers on why my life isn't progressing. She told me someone in my life is holding me back, so I narrated what happened between me and Glory to her. She said that ritual didn't work, and Glory is still taking my glory.'

Etim sat back and took a long look at his friend. He wanted to ask a lot of questions like why he went about seeking a prophetess over a solution which lay in his own hands. He wanted to ask what he had done within the last years to improve his life. He wanted to ask if his life had been any better before he met Glory. But he remembered that prophetesses do not lie and said instead, 'I can't believe this is happening all over again.'

'I should have seen it,' continued Omonigho, sighing, 'but she blinded my eyes and that of my family. Because now that I think about it, I did some foolish things that I normally wouldn't have done. Like when there was no food to eat in the house but when asked, I refused to go and buy things on credit in my name. Hours later, Glory came and complained of headache, I bought drugs on credit and food for her to eat.'

'That sounds like love,' he hid his sarcastic tone.'

'That was foolishness.'

Etim nodded.

'I also found out that she has had four abortions and none was mine, can you imagine?' Omonigho said with his eyes popping out.

'She had an affair with her brother-in-law and is a lesbian! How did I not see all these!?'

'Love is blind.'

'She blinded me,' Omonigho replied in a low furious voice. 'She blinded me and manipulated her way back into my life.'

'All this from just one girl!? Wow! It's sounds like something I'd watch in a movie.'

'I prayed with her, advised her, even defended her when people called her a witch and a whore. But what did she do? Nothing. She did worse things giving my enemies an opportunity to mock me.'

'Who else knows this?'

'No one. It is enough that people mock me just for walking beside her, how much more if this comes out in the open.'

'Yeah, true.'

Omonigho closed his eyes and a short silence followed. 'But I still love her,' he said, breaking the silence. 'I love our sex, her ravishing appetite for more. How she always knows what I want and how I want it.' Etim shook his head in dismay and wanted to speak when in the same breath Omonigho said, 'Who knows maybe during sex she invites her coven, because the deeper we go, the more she yearns for more.'

'You should be thankful she didn't get pregnant for you. You'd have been trapped for life.'

'Thankfully so. It shows God is with me,' he said with a nod.

Etim heaved a sigh. 'What else did the prophetess say?'

'The prophetess has put me through deliverance and prayers, and has asked me to pay an amount to use in buying some items for a cleansing ritual. She assures me that when she is done, I'll not recognise

Glory again. She'd look like a mad woman,' he said with determination in his eyes. 'But I don't want the love of my life to suffer.'

'Are you confused or are you mad?' asked Etim but Omonigho didn't reply, he was staring lost into the air. 'The first ritual didn't work because she is too powerful. What if the same thing happens again?' Etim asked.

'I would show her why some nicknamed me the devil.'

Etim frowned, uncomfortable with the tone of his voice. 'Meaning?'

'I will end it once and for all.'

'Just make sure this time you don't accuse her of being a witch again. Break up and move on. No calls, chats or visits. Unless you want to have this witch conversation again in another two years.'

A week after that conversation, Omonigho went missing and his family assumed Glory had finally fed him to her coven as their every attempt to reach her, too, was futile. It was on the 9 o'clock news they learnt Omonigho had been arrested by the police having choked a woman named Glory Edewor to death while making love to her, and having confirmed her death, he made love to her dead body repeated times as revealed by the autopsy.

Omonigho didn't hear what the judge said, but it caused a stir in the public as they murmured in intensifying whispers. In the chaos, Omonigho swivelled to the corner and at the far end of one of the benches for the public just by the entrance, he saw Glory. Glory stopped whispering to her neighbour and turned to him, and slowly she began to laugh at him.

'Stop laughing at me,' Omonigho shouted at her but Glory kept laughing. 'I said stop laughing,' he shouted again and there was silence in the courtroom. All turned in his direction to see who he was pointing at. 'You witch,' he continued to bark. 'I know who you are, I know what you are.'

The judge gestured to an officer to restrain him. The officer got there in time to prevent Omonigho from jumping out of the dock in a fit of rage.

'She is sitting right there and laughing at me,' Omonigho said to the judge.

'Who is?'

'Glory.'

There was a loud gasp from the public, and the judge shook his head. Omonigho's lawyer quickly got to his feet and said, 'Your honour, this is an example of insanity as I had earlier stated. My client is—'

'Do not say whatever it is you intend to say,' the judge cut in. 'Just sit and listen to my judgement.'

'I will, my lord, but I want to point out that my client is insane to go through with whatever punishment you must have—'

'Do you want to listen to my judgement on your seat or behind bars?' asked the judge, now furious.

'I am sorry, your honour,' Omonigho's lawyer nodded and sat. 'His acting was nice though,' he whispered.'

'I wasn't acting,' Omonigho whispered back. 'I saw her.'

His lawyer feigned a grin and returned his face to the judge.

'Whoever disturbs this hearing again will spend the next forty hours in a cell,' the judge ordered and silence ensued. 'Having heard all evidence put forward by the defence and the prosecution, and having listened to the jurors, this is my verdict. Omonigho Ogbamremu is guilty of first-degree murder and is therefore sentenced to death by hanging.'

The judge hit his gavel and the bailiff shouted:

'All rise.'

All rose except Omonigho. His soul died.

UNSHAPED GOLD

'I am not free while any woman is unfree, even if the shackles are very different from my own'

— Audre Lorde

'Since day one, a woman's already had everything she needs within herself, it's the world that convinced her she did not.'

— Rupi Kaur

The best part of Christmas was having to go to the village, yet I always dreaded the long and quiet hours of the four hundred and thirty kilometres it took to journey there. What made it worse was that we had to wake in the icy hours of the morning when dews were yet to decide whether to settle on the green grasses or just suspend themselves in the clouds. Though I loathed it, I was becoming accustomed to my parents waking us at four in the morning, but not my three siblings, they managed to go back to sleep for at least another thirty minutes which aroused Mother's anger.

Everything about Umuolu village was rich and beautiful, its cultural heritage laden with endless tales of how the world had changed for the worse. Being born and bred in the city of Lagos had given me a first-hand prospect to witness those changes. There was also something evocative about the way and manner in which they spoke their local language, Ukwani as it is called. Maybe because I could barely speak except for the greetings and simple words I had learnt from my parents, like *sepuru* which meant good morning and *nduwu-koma* meaning I'm fine. My inability to communicate in Ukwani often hampered my conversations, yet didn't deter me from wanting to speak.

I could never have enough of *Mmanwu* festival which celebrates the spirits of the dead and the great ancestors of the land. Every year the spirit chooses a man to dance the dance of the gods for an entire day; a man usually chosen from the age of seventeen and above. It was 2007, the first time I came across a dancing masquerade during the *Mmanwu* festival. I had always imagined masquerades to be towering and colossal in size – at least from the stories and folklore grandma told. This masquerade was short, covered in thick, red, beaded cloths, with an ugly wooden mask that kept his face a secret. I wondered for weeks how the men behind those masks could see through the vagueness and still dance with copious vigour like dancing palm trees. After several weeks of futile deliberation, I asked my father and he said, 'It is not the man that dances, but the spirit that possesses him.'

Asking father was worse. I had sleepless nights for years wondering and dreading that if I was a man chosen to wear the masquerade, the spirits would possess me. Growing up and listening to grandma's supernatural tales always got me petrified. In as much as they did, those stories made me feel like I belonged to a group of a culturally awoken teenagers, like I was a part of something bigger, like it was a life I had once lived or experienced. As I got older, I realised it felt like all of the above because of the texture of her tone when she told those stories, her strident pitched voice heightening each moment of implausible action, and the lush atmosphere she evoked. It made sense now.

We often would go back to school to share the most bizarre experiences and stories witnessed during our travels, and, those who didn't have stories to tell, they either listened to ours or – they had no choice than to listen. It soon became a contest of who told the most interesting of stories, and Uche didn't once lose the crown to another person. I could tell she made up the stories of old women with three legs who ate newborn babies every first and last day of the year, or old women who never smiled because they were witches and if ever they did smile at you, it meant they would suck your blood within the next seven days. Made-up or not, they were hilarious. It made me think all old hostile-looking women were inauspicious and witches, except for my grandma – I couldn't think of her as such even if I wanted to. She had the sweetest of smile, and a funny voice – especially when she recounted her tales and folklores – it was always something weird and funny which made us laugh, except for Gold Onyema, my long-time friend from Umuolu, who barely shared in our humour.

After every holiday, with a desire to take the crown off Uche, I wished I had the most bizarre story to tell, until I did, and then I wished I didn't. In recalling my last visit to the village, I was no longer taken aback by the petrifying old women who at every opportunity threw their hands into my fluffy hair, rubbing and asking me if I had woken up while I stood in front of them greeting *sepuru*. Nor was I perplexed by the old perverts – men of my father's age – who stole to the riverbank to peek at young girls taking their bath. The whispers of ugly pot-bellied men rumoured to have married the most beautiful women from neighbouring villages using *Juju* to capture these women's heart was no longer hilarious, neither was the controversial news of a man who had drowned about the same time of my birth and who, sixteen years later, was alive of the same age as when he drowned, bewildering. The man who went swimming and came out deaf and dumb no longer stole my sleep, even though it was rumoured he saw a mermaid who took his ability to see and speak so he would not reveal their secret to the world. I had assumed hearing of a wicked king who was buried alive by the villagers would usher in an era to see the end of the evil of men in Umuolu, but the story of Gold, my dear friend, proved otherwise. If only I hadn't learnt of her experience at night beneath the crescent moon, I perhaps would have slept it away after a day or two as I had other stories.

The evil she went through made me count my blessings as the Bible instructs. Having been born in a city saved me from the manacle of a culture which shoves women into the wallows of a never-ending pit. Howbeit Lagos is no holy ground where the girl-child can exist boundless of discrimination, it is however no comparison to a tradition which stiffens women. Grandma often in her tales made mention of how men saw their girl-child as a commodity, a way to settle old debts, a means to an end. She often would say, 'You don't know how lucky you are to have a mother who wanted more from life, and married a man who was willing to support her dream. Most young girls who grew up in the village with parents who knew no better only wished to marry a strong healthy man, and birth lots of children. Birthing large numbers of children was how they became proud women.'

I was probably thirteen or fourteen when I came across Nwakaego on one of our Christmas trips to the village. She was often talked about as the girl that would marry the strongest and richest man in the village because of her unique brown eyes and beautiful curves. All the other girls envied her except Gold, also young and beautiful, whom people thought would marry the next best man after Nwakaego, but Gold did not care about any of that, she had other plans for her life.

The first time I met Gold Onyema was three holidays ago in the wake of Boxing Day. It was more of a final preparation for *Mmanwu* festival the next day, and the majority of the people gathered spoke *Ukwani*. I sat upon a green wide leaf gathered from the gigantic tree under which I sat, twisting both ways in an attempt to discern who was who, and with any luck know which man would wear the masquerade's costume. My inability to speak Ukwani made my mission difficult. Every so often, I'd feign a chuckle at something someone said; it didn't matter that I didn't understand what was said, so long as everybody laughed, I was safe.

'I know,' came a voice from behind.

I looked up to see a figure standing above me, distorting the rays of the scorching sun. In the ambiguity, I could tell it was a female, but it wasn't until she asked if she could sit beside me and sat, did I get a full glimpse of her beauty. Her eyes were small and so was her mouth. Everything about her was small but suggestive and attractive. The only thing big about her were her breasts, probably too big for the body carrying them.

'You must be from Lagos city?' asked the stranger.

'How did you know?' I asked.

'It's always easy to spot a city girl when they visit,' she giggled.

I joined her in giggling, and at the end of it, she stretched out her hand and with a wide grin said, 'I am Gold Onyema. Pleased to meet you.'

I shifted my gaze back to the dwindling crowd around me; they seemed more guarded now in what they were saying. Even if I had understood Ukwani, their low-pitched voice made eavesdropping difficult.

'I know you don't understand Ukwani. I noticed you only laugh when everybody laughs,' Gold said.

I chuckled. 'I'm hoping you know who will wear the masquerade costume tomorrow then?'

Gold leaned towards me and whispered, 'You cannot know until tomorrow morning when the gods will possess a man of their choosing.'

I tried to hold back my laughter, but instead I ended up bursting out laughing. She sounded so much like Grandma when she told her supernatural tales.

'You don't believe me?' she asked.

'What can I say! Up until last year, I believed Boxing Days were meant for people to box each other.'

We went on to talk about everything and anything. I found her intelligence enthralling for someone born in the village. She spoke of how she wished she had a city life, and shared ideas of how to make the world a better place against my claim the world was too bad to be made better. Her dreams were bigger than Umuolu, bigger than the dream itself, and she had got used to being told that she was thinking too big. I went home that night to tell Grandma about her, and Grandma smiled. It was a smile of approval.

I began looking forward to every Christmas holiday in Umuolu. Gold would often take me round the village, then we would go to settle in her house until the cloak of the night where I listened to her speak, using words that I did not understand. One time, Nwakaego asked her what she wanted to be in the future, to which Gold replied, 'Environmental engineer.' Nwakaego and I looked at each other in a brief exchange of bemusement.

'Why?' Nwakaego asked.

I was very sure that, like me, Nwakaego didn't know who or what an environmental engineer did, but she didn't want to be outshone by a girl whom she considered second after her, only in beauty.

'The quality of air is depreciating, the soil and rivers are polluted because of the oil spillages. As an environmental engineer, my primary focus will be to find solutions to water-borne diseases, wastewater management and air pollution.'

'You always have an answer for everything,' Nwakaego said, nodding in feigned understanding.

After she left, I said out loud to Gold and in her mother's hearing, 'Beauty without brains.' We laughed.

Last year's Christmas was the first time we didn't travel to the village. Father had some business dealings that stole his time and therefore ours too. I couldn't help but think about all I had missed; from the elders speaking in their sexy Ukwani language, to the masquerade possessed by the spirits and shaking his feet to the near-rusty leather drums of *Mmanwu* festival. I missed Gold, but maybe I missed more the *big-big* words that always came out of her mouth.

Christmas holiday soon came again and I began counting down to the day we would travel. I spent half of the previous night imagining what I had missed, and the new adventure that awaited me. I became too impatient to sleep and too keen to begin the journey.

'This is surprising,' said Mother as she entered my room on the morning we were to travel to the village. I had taken my bath and was dressed, ready for the journey.

I looked at the wall clock; the short hand was on four and the long hand was just settling on twelve. I had woken almost an hour earlier.

'Wake your brothers up and get them ready,' she instructed.

'Yes, ma.'

'Don't you feel cold?' she asked.

'Not really.'

'Hmmm!' she studied me carefully. 'Wake your brothers,' she instructed and left.

I waited for her to leave the room then sprinted to the window to close it, wondering how I hadn't realised it was open and I was cold. Within the next thirty minutes, my brothers were down by the car, looking sharp and ready. I was confident that one if not all three of my brothers had cursed me for waking them instead of their mother which was customary. They got their revenge in my frown when I began to complain father was driving slow. We didn't arrive in Umuolu until late at night.

At the break of dawn, I greeted whoever I could but didn't wait for anyone to throw their hands into my fluffy hair while asking an obvious question. I hurried to Gold's compound. Her mother sat on a three-legged wooden stool. She hid her face on seeing me and I was sure I saw her wiping tears off her face.

'Good morning, ma,' I greeted. I was standing opposite her now.

'When did you arrive?' she struggled to sound excited.

I could sense the uneasiness in her voice, like she had been crying. I would ask Gold why, I thought.

'Last night, ma. If it wasn't so late, I'd have made my way down here.'

She managed a grin. Her lips quaked and the grin couldn't hold for long. It was obvious she had been crying.

'Ma, is Gold sleeping already?' I asked, stretching my neck towards the house. 'Gold! Better run out here. Your big sister is here,' I joked.

The cotton hanging above the front door shook and Obi, Gold's younger brother, hurried out.

'Obi!' I called in excitement. 'How have you been?'

'Fine,' was his brief reply.

He didn't share the same joy in seeing me as I had in seeing him. He was clad in short knickers and a brown singlet. It was how he always dressed, the whole village knew him. His way of dressing didn't make him popular, his menacing attitude to people – old or young —– did. He was the complete opposite of his sister. They were so opposite that when I learnt he was Gold's brother, I asked if they were related by blood.

'He is flesh and blood,' Gold had replied, 'and I love him even though he's my naughty little brother.'

I grinned. I had no choice than to love him too, but we barely crossed paths.

'Where is your sister? Tell her I am around,' I said again. He stood motionless. 'Did you hear what I said, Obi?'

Obi didn't reply. He moved back and cast a piercing gaze at me, shifted his gaze to his mother and walked away.

I was disgusted by his action; I had always heard he was that way and worse, but seeing him act in such a manner hit differently. His mother soon burst into loud uncontrollable tears as she watched her son walk out of the compound. How could a boy his age be so disrespectful? I said beneath my breath.

'Nne, stop crying. It's all right,' I said with assurance, but it ended up arousing in her more tears. 'Please tell Gold that I am around. I'll come back later,' I said and left.

I walked home that evening with so many questions in my head. Where is Gold? Is she being punished for something? Did she choose not to see me? Is she sick? Did she travel? I couldn't put a stay to my thoughts, but what made it worse were the crazy imaginings that crawled into my mind. I shoved them aside and headed straight to Grandma.

There was urgency in my steps as I dashed into her room.

Grandma looked tired and was attempting to sleep.

'Grandma,' I called and sat next to her. 'I went to Gold's house but didn't see her. Maybe she doesn't want to see me. When last did you see her?'

Grandma sighed, then sat up. She first leaned against the wall, her eyes heavy with words. I knew something was wrong, that was her sign when she was about to give bad news.

'Gold is helping to continue her family's name. She is a very strong girl,' Grandma said.

'Helping to continue her family's name!?' I whispered. 'Oh,' I lifted my gaze to Grandma. 'Did she get the scholarship? She did mention to me the last time we saw that she would be applying for a scholarship. I'm really happy she got it.'

Grandma said nothing, but there was pity in her eyes.

'Did she get the scholarship?' I asked, more curious.

'She did, but her father wasn't willing to support her.'

'Then what do you mean by she's continuing her family's name?' I asked, looking confused.

'The Onyema family have been under a generational curse,' Grandma said. 'This curse makes all their first-born sons go mad when they get to a certain age.'

'Gold's father has gone mad?' I asked, curious.

'No. He is the second son of his father so the curse evaded him.'

'Thank God,' I said, then paused. 'Wait, Obi is the first son of his father. Is he going to run mad?'

'He was supposed to,' Grandma said and heaved a sigh. 'But not anymore.'

'They found a cure!?' I asked with excitement.

'Yes,' Grandma answered, but by the way she looked at me, I could tell there was something unpleasant she wasn't telling me.

'Grandma, what about Gold? When last did you see her?' I asked.

'A long time ago.'

'What do you mean by a long time ago, Grandma?'

'Gold has taken the honour of saving her family name,' Grandma said.

After long seconds of silence, Grandma went on to narrate how Obi was almost at the age when the curse was to take root in him, and being the only son, his father would not have it – this made the rumours that he often blamed and fought his wife for not birthing more sons true – so he went about visiting native doctors for a cure but there was none. He then decided Gold would carry the curse for Obi, so the latter could live on to carry the family's name. It was painful to know that the brother she loved despite his shortcomings didn't object to her carrying the curse of madness for him. He even joined in tricking her to the herbalist's shrine where the ritual was performed and ever since that night, she had been mad.

I was lost for words; beyond rage that all the village elders supported putting a curse on a bright girl-child in place of a despicable son because their tradition was one in which the male child were more valuable than the female child. The male child evoked respect, strength and dignity as they continued the family name, while the female children were nothing but properties, meant to be inherited by sons, uncles, brothers, and anything subject to the patriarchy. The girl-child was assumed to be in transit, as she would eventually marry and thus lose all the identities that made her a member of the family she was born into. Nothing mattered more to an Igbo man than his family name.

I lay back in utmost silence as tears rolled down my eyes; it was as if the world should stop spinning. It was difficult to tell if I was saddened by the thought of the endless pain my dear Gold was suffering, or because she was a victim of a patriarchal society where women played important roles (contributing to and stabilising the family and society), but being women, were taken to be valueless and controllable.

'Your tears will solve nothing,' said Grandma.

'B…b-b-but…' I found myself speechless. The pain in my heart was too heavy for my words to come forth.

After some minutes, with tears still in my eyes, I asked, 'Why didn't the women come together to stop it? Are we not supposed to have a voice? How can you all sit and watch the life of a promising girl cut short, just to save a worthless boy who is nothing but a nuisance to the society and his family?'

'He may be a nuisance, but he is still a man.'

'It doesn't change that he is worthless. And his father,' I raged.

'Are you aware that your younger siblings are more valuable than you are?' Grandma said, and I could tell from the tone of her voice that she was sincere.

'No, Grandma. I do not need some old rotten culture to tell me who I am or who I am not, neither do my values lie in the words of vile men. I am a woman, and if I do not know who or what I am, then I am not worthy to be called a woman.'

Grandma let out a sheepish smile, revealing half of her brown broken teeth. She reflected for some seconds and chuckled lightly.

'My child. You are born in a time where people grow far away from their culture, and so you would not understand who or what a woman should be. A woman is more beautiful and adored when she pleases a man. In fact, the essence of her life is to please a man. In your modern eye, you may think of it as stupidity that women are not born to inherit but to be inherited. Our forefathers cannot be wrong; they were guided by the gods. What a child sees standing, an elder sees sitting.'

I wanted to tell her how everything she had said was wrong, how women from time immemorial had been programmed to think a certain way, and how such programming had done more harm than good, yet I didn't. Trying to convince her against her will was foolishness, she would regardless be of the same opinion still.

'It is sad what your friend is going through,' Grandma said, 'At least be happy that you're free from the shackles of…'

'Free!? No, Grandma,' I retorted. 'I am not free while any woman is unfree, even if the shackles are very different from mine,' I fumed to my feet. 'And neither are you,' I added and banged the door behind me.

My bed became my solace. I spent the rest of my holiday locked in my room. My brothers often alternated bringing me food, and when they returned, they found the dish they had served earlier staring them back in the face. Every trick in the book to get me outside my room failed. I refuse to feign politeness to a group of people – men who are heartless and women who are voiceless to not acknowledge the agony forced upon them, and stand against it.

Before our journey back to Lagos, I stole into the dark night to Gold's compound, to see her mother. Her eyes had not ceased from incessant tears; they had swollen to the extent there was nothing else left to swell. There was nothing to say, the silence in both our tears said it all.

I could never forget the silence that swept through the classroom after I had narrated to them my dear Gold's ordeal. It was obvious I had taken the crown off Uche – after several years of attempts, but it didn't matter anymore, the pain in my heart wouldn't let me wear a crown that was won on the victory of defeat. A defeat to Gold, a defeat to all women.

It has been thirty years since I last visited Umuolu. Everything about that place died in me that night, it was the last time I ever heard Grandma's stories. Her thrilling voice which always sounded funny was no longer funny. I was never bothered if her brown scattered teeth had changed coloru, nor what her face now looked like. When the news of her death came, I cried, but I refused to attend her burial. If she had hoped her death would be the reason I visited Umuolu once more, she failed.

I began to see the world in a different way after that night. The world was in twos: light and dark, white and black, the good and the bad, justice and inequality, kindness and evil, love and hate, men and women. I once heard a man say 'The world is in a balance of scale, and one cannot outweigh the other.' He must have thought himself intelligent by reason of his philosophy, but beneath his belief was foolishness and a pure denial of the truth that from the beginning of the world, nothing was ever balanced. It had always been light versus dark, white versus black, the good versus the bad, justice versus inequality, kindness versus evil, love versus hate, and women versus men. The scale, against nature's will, often favours the latter(s), and it is upon this unfairness the world thrives. My aunt once said the only thing that makes life unfair is the delusion that it should be fair. I was too young to understand at the time, but now I do.

I was at my office when I received the call informing me of Gold's passing; I was too downhearted and dumb to reply. I couldn't shake away the caller's voice long after the call had ended echoing, 'Gold died yesterday. I'm sorry.' Between the call informing me of her death, and her actual death, I couldn't tell which bore more pain. I fell back into my chair, raked my hands into my hair, threw my face back to stare into the white formless ceiling in an attempt not to cry, but those silent tears, as they did many years ago, rolled down my face. I refused to reach for my hanky, or the tissue that rested by the corner of my desk. I wanted my tears to flow hoping they would in turn heal me, but they didn't. These last thirty years were proof that whoever advised we shed tears because they heal, lied. Tears are my silent form of grief; the words I could not speak.

Gold died free. Free from the thoughts of how wicked a world she lived in. Free from the knowledge that she was in a mental state of psychiatric disorder brought upon her by cultural misogyny, an egotistical father and a churlish brother whom she dearly loved. She was free from the shackles of a system that was designed to fail her from its inception, free from a world of misogyny and patriarchy in the disguise of fairness. If anything, she was in a better place.

I dreaded receiving the call of her death, and when I did it soured my day. I soon became livid then aggrieved on recalling that her father few years ago had hanged himself. His action must have been born from a concealed agony and regret having let himself be fooled by his pride and culture. If nothing, his choice of death by hanging brought a deserved end to a miserable life. His stupid son, Obi, couldn't have made his miserableness any worse. He became a nuisance, a menace to the community. I heard he died too but in a shameful way.

'Ma,' came the voice of my secretary, who had just walked into my office. 'The documents you requested are here.'

I said nothing, still lost in my pain and anger.

'Are you okay, ma?' she asked.

I feigned a smile, and gestured she drop the file on my desk. She did, and was almost at the door when she swivelled.

'That reminds me. George called. He said he has been trying to reach you but your number is switched off.'

I gasped and looked to my phone. I must have switched it off after the call.

'Okay. I'll call him back,' I said.

'Ma, you don't look okay. Are you sure you're okay?'

A part of me wanted to yell at her and stone her out of my office, but the shrewdness in me knew she was only bothered and wanted to be of help.

I looked up at her for the first time since she walked into my office.

'I'm fine, Jumoke. Thank you.'

Jumoke grinned and strode out of my office. It was at that point I had noticed she was clad in a short red skirt. I should have asked if she had a date later tonight, or if she wore the short skirt because she had said her long skirts were not attracting men her way. She had revealed this to me at last year's end-of-the-year party, after inviting her to my office for a drink. We laughed over a lot of things, until she got drunk and asked why I wasn't married.

'Does it matter?' I asked.

'I think it does. With what and who you've become, a man in your life might just be what you need for people to truly respect you.'

'Why do you think so?' I winced.

'It's the way it has been since time immemorial,' she answered, paused for some seconds then chuckled.

I poured her another drink. Most people speak their truth when drunk.

'I won't be surprised if men are avoiding you because of what you have,' Jumoke continued. 'Maybe you should humble yourself and try not to have some of the things you have,' she giggled out loud.

I laughed too because of the manner in which she uttered those words and not because what she said made any sense.

'I think that's why your ex left,' Jumoke said with confidence. 'He was insecure about you having more than him.'

'I am not worried about intimidating men,' I said to her, and a part of me wondered why I was trying to explain to a drunk. 'The type of man who will be intimidated by me is exactly the type of man I have no interest in.'

Jumoke let out a burst of laughter at the end of my sentence. In the five years she had been my secretary, I had never seen her that alive, probably because I had never seen her drunk.

She lifted her drink and yelled, 'To a woman who doesn't give a fuck.'

'Jumoke!' I said. 'Would you someday like to have all what I have, and more?'

She paused for a few seconds, mulled over it, then said, 'Who wouldn't?'

I let out a soft grin and sipped from my glass of champagne, hoping she could hear the betrayal in her desire.

'But if I do,' she continued, 'I may never have a man.' She laughed and gulped her last glass of champagne. 'I think your man ... George, is it? I think he suits you. He is...'

Everything she said from that point fizzled. In that instant, she spoke like my grandmother. I could not bear listening to a woman speak less of herself, one who only sees her value and worth through the myopic pupils of a man. She was one of those with unfounded conclusions that I shunned men because I was too proud to be with a man, or worse, could never submit to a man. I had long lost interest in making an effort to explain what was true and what wasn't, chiefly since I learnt people never changed the opinions they have of you. There was a reason people didn't see the world as black and white, but as black or white. Those reasons were born out of experience, experience birthed from pain.

My phone rang, intruding on my reminiscing. It was George. I didn't realise I had switched the phone back on.

'Hey babe,' I said after I picked up.

'Hi,' said George. 'I have been trying to reach you. Did your secretary deliver my message?'

'Yeah she did.'

There was a long pause at the other end of the phone.

'What's wrong, baby? First your phone was off and now you sound sad. Talk to me.'

I heaved a sigh, wondering whether to tell him what had happened or just lie that I was fine. Lying was easier.

'I am just tired,' I said.

'Hmm. I think I know a little of you to know the difference between when you sound tired, and when you're sad.'

I chuckled, still uncertain how he could tell the difference. He must know me so well.

'My aunt called to say Gold... you remember her, don't you?'

'Yeah. Your friend from the village.'

'Yes. She died yesterday.'

'Sorry to hear that. I know what she meant to you.'

I had stopped crying. My tears had become too weak, and the chilly air from the air conditioner on the wall dried my eyes.

'Yeah,' I whispered in an effort not to unleash my tears.

'Sorry I'm not there with you. I wish I was.'

I heaved a sigh and closed my eyes. The picture in my head was George's broad shoulder and his burly chest, a safe haven to rest my head and lay my thoughts. He too loved those moments and didn't conflicts my thoughts by filling them with his opinions. He'd wait till I was ready to talk and all he'd do was listen. He only ever gave his opinions when I asked for them. He once said to me, 'When women say a man is a good conversationalist, what they actually mean is that he is a good listener. Women love to be listened to.'

'I wish I was with you too,' I finally said.

'I wanted to ask if you'd be free for dinner tonight, but I guess not today.'

'It's fine,' I cut in. 'What time?'

'Is eight okay by you?'

'Yeah, it is.'

'See you later then. Bye.'
'Bye.'

I spent the majority of the first hour of our dinner date reiterating to George everything he had heard me say about Gold, and to my surprise, he didn't interrupt me. I wasn't a fool to think he was a very patient man, but I liked him because he knew when he needed to assume the virtue of patience.

'Sorry,' I said, after my long soliloquy about Gold. 'I know I bore you with my pain.'

He chuckled and casted a long gaze at me. 'I wouldn't be so nice to claim some parts of it weren't boring.'

I giggled.

'You needed to let them out,' he continued, 'and I was your ear. Why else do I have a big ear,' he joked.

We laughed and I pinched his ear. We ate on.

'Is it just me, or is this rice tasteless?' I asked.

He shifted his gaze from me to his plate of fried Chinese rice and back to me, nodded his head and said, 'It is definitely just you.'

We laughed again.

'I initially wanted for us to have *Amala*, your favourite,' he said in an enthusiastic voice. 'Then I thought swallowing *Amala* and *ewedu ati gbegiri* while telling me a sad story won't make a good combination,' he said with amusement in his voice.

I shook my head, stared at him with admiration. He was cute, stubborn and considerate at the same time. I often told him he was just too perfect, to which he always replied 'I am not perfect, and no man can be perfect.' His perfection wasn't in that he did everything right and never made me feel angry or sad, but that he believed in women's rights, and didn't exercise control over me like I was his property or an object to be inherited. He respected me like a woman should be, and I did likewise. There were days when we disagreed and refused to speak to one another, but ended up sneaking to our WhatsApp and Facebook accounts to check each other's page to see who was online, hopefully waiting for the other to send a message first. We always laughed about this when we returned to speaking terms.

I remember the first time he asked to be my boyfriend. His words were brazen and direct, but he later confessed that he must have rehearsed those words a thousand times before he opened his mouth. Not that he was intimidated, but the things he had heard people claim of me made him a bit self-conscious. I asked why he went ahead to ask me out regardless of the discouraging words he heard of me, and he replied, 'Only the brave deserves the fair.' I didn't even say yes to his request to go out with him before I kissed him. I gave him the answer to his request after our first sex at his place, and after I said yes, we covered ourselves beneath the bedsheets again. I liked the way he treated his mother and his sisters, he respected his friends too. I had told him I wanted a relationship without commitment, and he smiled. 'It'd be difficult,' he said, then gave a long pause to wonder what it really meant. 'I think I know what you mean. It is achievable, that is if you don't fall to my charm,' he boasted. He was right, I fell.

A waitress arrived at our table with a dessert trolley and I joggled out of my memories.

'Ma,' the waitress said, 'this is for you.'

'I didn't order anything,' I said out loud.

I looked at George and he shrugged.

The waitress flashed me a warm smile and walked back to her station.

'What is going on?' I asked George.

'I don't know,' he winced. 'At least open it to find out what is in it.'

I removed the lid from the trolley and revealed a small fanciful cake with something yellow planted neatly at the top. I leaned closer; it was a wedding ring. I gasped and looked at George; he was on one knee.

'I practised in front of my mirror what to say and how to say it, but truth is, I would be lying if I tell you I perfected my speech. I do not know any other way to say it, but I want to spend the rest of my life with you. Will you marry me?'

I chuckled. Seeing him on one knee made him more adorable. I lifted my left hand mid-air, he reached towards it and positioned the ring with all sense of courtesy onto my middle finger. I grinned in admiration of the sparkling gold steel that beautified my hand. I looked down to him and he was still on one knee, his eyes keenly waiting for an answer.

'Oh dear! I thought I had said yes already,' I joked.

He almost chuckled, but didn't. I guess he wanted to keep the moment as official and formal as he could. I stood and lifted him to his feet.

'Yes babe, I will be your wife.'

We embraced, and the sound of our lips meeting was lost in the reverberating echoes of the applause around us.

DROWN

To the brave Igbo souls that chose the sea over slavery, your resilience became the first march to freedom for slavers. You gave the world an Igbo landing when you
DROWNED.

Did you want to see me broken?
Bowed head and lowered eyes?
Shoulders falling down like teardrops,
Weakened by my soulful cries?
I'm a black ocean, leaping and wide,
Welling and swelling I bear in the tide.
I am the dream and the hope of the slave.
I rise.
I rise.
I rise.

Maya Angelou

IN THE YEAR 1803. APRIL–MAY.

The sun was beginning to set when Chijioke's dead body was carried out from the death chamber by four able-bodied men, all gritting their teeth against the green leaf in their mouths. The men moved in quick calculated steps like they were in a hurry to drop off the body as a result of the pain of lifting Chijioke on mahogany planks tied together with palm leaves hardened by the dry winds from the north.

An abrupt silence swept through as the pallbearers carrying Chijioke entered Nwokeoma Nduka's compound. The son of the soil has arrived, their silence said. Nwokeoma rose at the sight of his son's body being lifted into where would have been his inheritance had his life not been cut short. Nwokeoma heaved a heavy sigh, then scanned around the compound just as the woman behind him wiped her tearful face in a hurry before her abomination was discovered. The pallbearers placed the body on the high bush table standing at the middle of the compound beside a deep extensive grave, next to which lay Chijioke's notable belongings: hunting gun, spear, small native knife, bow and arrow, all to be buried with him.

Ugommaeze rose and hurried to see her brother's face one last time before he was covered with cloths, strings, Manilla and young palm leaves all symbolising rebirth – in the hope of his reincarnation, but she knew her brother would never be born again. Others might think he would, but her grief wouldn't let her believe in a long standing culture belief. Her Nne, Omasirichi, scuttled after her. She too wanted to see her son's face before he was covered and laid in the ground.

'I want to cry too,' Omasirichi said, looking into her daughter's eyes, 'but you should try your best not to. Nobody forgives a woman who commits an abomination by weeping during a burial, even if it were the burial of her only brother.'

Ugommaeze nodded at Nne in despair at her powerlessness to weep for her only brother. She looked towards her Nna, his face scrawled with sorrow. His eyes were sore; he was managing to stand strong. Ugommaeze looked around the compound over the crowd that had assembled to send her brother to his new home, and only a few men cried, their tears not enough to soak the ground. In that instance, Ugommaeze hated that women were forbidden to cry during the burial rites of a deceased, so as to allow his spirit to leave this life in peace. The consequence of a woman crying was that the woman would sacrifice a goat or fowl at the feet of the corpse in order to purify the stain of her tears. It baffled Ugommaeze still that men who were allowed to cry were however warned not to bewail to excess the loss of a young soul as this put the soul in danger of drowning in excessive tears on its way to heaven.

Nwokeoma joined his wife and daughter, all three now staring at Chijioke. With sadness in his eyes, Nwokeoma motioned to the high Chief to come forward and say a thing or two before Chijioke was finally put into the ground. The high Chief stepped forward, and began to speak about the deceased, and how Chukwu would welcome Chijioke's soul into heaven for his deeds while on earth.

Ugommaeze turned her face away from the high Chief hoping to be distracted by anything or anyone. The high Chief's speech bored her as he spoke about heaven and one's chi. The deceased's father should do the honour of speaking at his child's funeral rather than a high Chief – who is also a well-known drunkard – paid to speak at every funeral because he was a Chief who was high. If her Nna wasn't two years behind in age, he would have been the oldest in Aro village, making him the high Chief.

Ugommaeze stared into the heaven which the high Chief has been speaking about; the sun was no longer in view. The cloud had completely swallowed the sun, but the air was still warm and the breeze gentle. It was in such hours her brother would have been returning with the spoil from his hunt: a big grasshopper or a tubby antelope on good days, and on bad days a scrawny rabbit or nothing at all. He often had more good than bad days, and he was celebrated on either day. He was loved, the entire Nnduka family was loved and they had their father to thank for that. She couldn't bear to look at her brother being carried down. She turned her face away, but the sighs and sorrowful sounds from mourners stimulated in her a mental image of Chijioke being covered with sands.

Ugommaeze moved her face over the compound, and there, standing by the entrance, to her surprise was Afamefuna, who with rapt attention watched as his friend Chijioke was being put into the ground. Ugommaeze's heart began to beat, in a good way, as she moved step by step behind the mourners. She fixed her gaze on Afamefuna until they both came in full view of one another, and without a word spoken aloud, their faces lit up with an amorous expression, like one or the other was a Sun which lit and enthused the other. She thought it unaccountable the way her emotions stirred with calm and her body prickled with fervour at the sight of the man she loved when she was supposed to be mourning, yet she worried more that there would be another death if her Nna saw Afamefuna. Afamefuna was audacious enough to dare to step into the compound, especially after the last incident, and Ugommaeze thought he was bold and daring. There is something sexy about a man's brazen-boldness which makes a woman drool over him.

'You came,' said Ugommaeze. Her voice was a little weak.

'He was my friend too.' Afamefuna's voice was placid.

Ugommaeze ran into his embrace and Afamefuna consoled her with gentle strokes across her back. His body was warm which made hers suddenly turn cold so she could stay long in his warmness.

'You know my Nna will kill you if he sees you here. You should leave before—'

'Nso!!' shouted a loud voice from behind the lovers.

Ugommaeze feared to turn towards the voice, as it was one she knew too well.

'Please, run,' she begged Afamefuna.

Afamefuna shook his head. He looked head-on at Nwokeoma who approached him with fury.

'Abomination!' shouted Nwokeoma again.

The closer Nwokeoma neared his daughter and Afamefuna, the more furious he became. He threw himself into the air and with a formed fist descended on the lovers, but Afamefuna was swift to dodge and escaped Nwokeoma's furious punch by an inch.

Ugommaeze was unsure who the punch was intended for, but glad that neither she nor Afamefuna was at the end of the punch of the strongest man in the village of Aro. She fell on her knee before her Nna.

'Nna, I can explain,' Ugommaeze pleaded.

'How dare you disrespect me and dishonour your late brother,' Nwokeoma raised his voice. He flashed Afamefuna a furious gaze then turned back to his daughter. 'You let this abomination come into my home!'

'It wasn't her fault,' Afamefuna stepped forward unflinching. 'I came to pay my respect to Chijioke. He was my friend too.'

'Tarrr!!!' Nwokeoma exclaimed. He threatened to throw his fist again at Afamefuna, but for the mourners who held him down. 'Amadioha strike your tongue there,' he cursed.

'Nna forgive us,' Ugommaeze held on to her father, tighter.

Nwokeoma cast a gaze of displeasure at her and hissed. He shifted his gaze back to Afamefuna.

'Leave this compound at once and stay away from my family,' Nwokeoma tried to sound calm, but he didn't look it. 'You won't be this lucky next time.' He spat and walked away.

Ugommaeze remained on her knee, face down, ashamed to look at her Nna or Afamefuna, but she heard people whispering to and urging Afamefuna to leave the compound, for they might be unable to hold back Nwokeoma if he made to strike again. Ugommaeze felt Afamefuna's palm land on her shoulder, and wished she could place hers above his for reassurance. Instead, she remained motionless and watched his footprints mark the sands till the marks disappeared.

Ugommaeze started up furiously to confront her Nna. As she approached his Ulo – the second biggest round-wall mud house in Aro – her anger dwindled when she looked up at its thatch roof. It was just two weeks ago when the roof had begun leaking that Chijioke reconstructed the whole thing with the help of Nna. First, they wove the skeletal framework of the roof with sliced bamboo poles which they then placed sloping down and crossed with palm fronds. Halfway through the reconstruction, Nne served them palm oil and roasted yam but Nna claimed it was laziness to eat while working so he alone knotted the rafters at various points to make them unbreakable while Chijioke ate. After eating, Chijioke joined Nna and they both covered the roof with dried grasses and fronds. It was the last time they were together as a family.

Ugommaeze reached to open the raffia door mat when she overheard her Nna and Nne arguing. She peeped in.

'What do you mean I should have acted differently?' Nwokeoma roared angrily. 'So what did you expect when the son of my enemy was bold enough to step into my compound, that I would welcome and offer him a seat!?' Nwokeoma snapped his fingers. 'Amadioha forbids! He was lucky not to have joined Chijioke today.'

'He doesn't have to be your enemy too.'

Nwokeoma flashed Omasirichi a menacing gaze.

'So now you defend him too!? Hmmm! As you could not sleep with his father, do you want to make up for it with his son!?'

Omasirichi didn't reply. She sat softly on a stool and stared speechless at her husband like she had something to say but didn't think it was worth being said.

For a brief moment, Nwokeoma wore a look of remorse. He was a typical traditionalist but unlike tradition expects, he loved his wife and had a soft spot for her. His pride, however, wouldn't allow him admit that he did.

'You still think I love him after all these years?' Omasirichi finally said after her long silence.

'Do you not?' Nwokeoma retorted. His voice had become gentle.

'I married you not him. The gods favoured you for a reason.'

'It is not like you had a choice. You loved him, he was who you wanted. You married me because I was available.' He reflected for a few seconds and said, 'I was lucky. The gods didn't favour me.'

Omasirichi made to speak, but instead heaved a heavy sigh and looked into the empty air.

'Why else did you not forbid your daughter from claiming to love his half-bastard son?' asked Nwokeoma with a dispirited tone which suggested he had pondered the question a thousand times.

'Afamefuna is not a bastard,' Omasirichi defended.

'You say it like you wished you bore him.'

'The thoughts of a jealous man.'

'Watch your tongue, woman,' Nwokeoma shot back.

'I shed tears sometimes,' Omasirichi said, almost tearful now. 'You dishonour me over a love which happened three generations ago.'

Nwokeoma said nothing. His silence said it all.

Ugommaeze seized the silence in the room and encroached upon the moment.

'Nna,' Ugommaeze announced her presence. 'I am not pleased with how you treated Afamefuna.'

'Will you shut up your dirty mouth before I remove your teeth,' Nwokeoma replied angrily. It was the rage intended for his wife. He was now on his feet as if ready to pounce on his daughter, but Nwokeoma would never lay his hand on a woman, much more his blood. Time after time he often said only weak men hit women to prove a point.

'Nna, you break my heart by disapproving of my love for Afamefuna.'

'You not only broke my heart the first day you told me you love him. Today, you dishonoured me and your brother by letting that fool into my compound.'

'He came to pay his last respects to his friend.'

'Tarrr!! I forbid that word from your mouth. My son, even in his grave, could never associate with a mere commoner.'

'That mere commoner is to thank on the many occasions Chijioke came home with big spoils from his hunt.'

'You lie,' Nwokeoma shot back

Ugommaeze shook her head slowly.

'You do not even respect the dead. You now speak ill of your brother in the name of love?' He scoffed and shifted his gaze to Omasirichi. 'I wonder who she inherited that from?'

'Chijioke was friends with Afamefuna and they often went hunting together. He made me promise to keep it a secret,' Ugommaeze said in one breath.

'You lie,' Nna blurted out in disbelief.

'Upon my brother's grave, I tell no lies.' Ugommaeze touched the ground with the tip of her finger, then touched her tongue with the same finger before lifting it into the air.

Nna sat back dumfounded trying to piece together the truth about what he had just heard. He would have claimed she told lies and spoke ill of her late brother for love, but the one thing he knew without doubt about her was that she never lied, except for the petty white lies she occasionally told at her young age to escape punishment.

'They both were together in his last hunt that ended his life,' she added, breaking the gloomy silence.

Nwokeoma rose with a sudden vigour as if struck by an idea, then in a throbbing triumphant tone of realisation said, 'That means he killed him. Afamefuna killed my son!'

'Nna!' Ugommaeze exclaimed. 'That was not what I said.'

'That was not what she said,' Omasirichi added.

'Aha!' Nwokeoma exclaimed. 'I see it now. Because Igwebuike could not kill me, he sent his son to become friends with mine and killed my lineage instead.' He let out a reflective sigh and cast his gaze into the heavens. 'An eye for an eye, a son for a son,' he said grimly.

'But Nna,' Ugommaeze spoke up, 'Chijioke died from a snakebite, we all saw the bite mark on his skin.'

'He fooled us to see what he wanted us to see. Afamefuna killed my son and placed a snake to bite him afterwards. Ha! HHHHhhh He will surely hang.'

'Nwokeoma,' Omasirichi called, 'you can't just spring accusations because you do not like a person.'

Nwokeoma made to walk away, completely ignoring his wife, then he felt something weigh him down. He looked at his feet and it was Ugommaeze.

'My child, you cannot understand. What an elder sees sitting, you cannot see standing.'

At that he pulled his leg away from Ugommaeze's grip and hurried out of the hut leaving her in tears.

'What have I done?' Ugommaeze cried. 'I have just doomed the man I love.'

'Forgive your Nna,' said Omasirichi. 'Losing a first son is losing one's pride. He will come to his senses soon.'

'No, Nne,' Ugommaeze wiped the tears from her face. 'We both know Nna is not the kind of man who lets go when he has a thought floating in his head.'

Omasirichi placed her palm on her daughter's shoulder. Ugommaeze sniffed and at once stopped crying as it dawned on her that Afamefuna too had placed his palm on her shoulder before he left. How could she have forgotten! In one stroke she wiped away the remaining tears from her face and swivelled to her mother. Her eyes widened with realisation, and without saying a word, she hurried out.

* * * *

The night was drawing nigh, but it wasn't close enough to prevent Ugommaeze from embarking on her daredevil walk to warn Afamefuna of the danger he was in. It has been more than an hour since Afamefuna had communicated to her that he would wait for her at their tryst by placing his palm on her shoulder; it was one of the ways they spoke in secret. She wondered if his patience would keep him waiting, or would have waned by the hour and made him head for his home.

Ugommaeze was about to cross the Ugboga junction when she saw Nwokeoma down the road walking with hurrying feet and heading in the direction of the high Chief's ulo. She hid till he was out of sight, then quickened her steps. Afamefuna was in a greater danger than she had imagined. Ugommaeze walked with quick feet but her thoughts were slow and heavy, her mind leaping from one thought to the other. First she wondered why Nna was possessed with a false notion about the death of his son, blinded by enmity that was born some more than twenty years ago, then she wondered why he didn't take his own advice that hate was a cloak which clogs a man's emotions.

Nwokeoma was blinded by his hate for Afamefuna's father, Igwebuike, his proclaimed arch-enemy. It was said in the corners of the village that Igwebuike and Omasirichi had been madly in love with each other. Luck ran out on their love when on the way to Umunna to declare his intentions to marry Omasirichi, Igwebuike along with his kinsmen by accident broke the calabash of fresh palm wine he was to give his future in-laws for their daughter. The breaking of the calabash was by tradition regarded as an omen of bad luck and such a suitor was to turn back immediately and desist from his plans to marry from that particular house. In Igwebuike's bid to try to prove that his intentions for Omasirichi were pure and noble, he went on to their Umunna and it was discovered that one of the plantain he had brought had two fingers – which was against their tradition as they believed that two fingers of plantain joined together was a bad omen. Igwebuike was reluctant to let go of the love of his life over some unfounded tradition and pressed his kinsmen not to return without the hand of the woman he loved. In Igwebuike's attempt to detach the conjoined plantain, he failed to carry out the act with his eyes closed, and thus saw the separation, which by tradition meant he would be the father of conjoined twins. His suit was rejected; three bad omens in one day was beyond bad luck.

Months later, Nwokeoma asked for Omasirichi's hand in marriage and all the rites were carried out without any bad omen. They got married, and in nine months the wailing of Chijioke roared out of their ulo. Igwebuike too moved on and got married, but it was rumoured his heart lay elsewhere for his wife never got the best part of it.

Anger brewed between both men for they were in love with the same woman, and Igwebuike being the strongest man in Aro at the time challenged Nwokeoma to a gidigbo fight. Mid-fight in their gidigbo contest, Igwebuike was informed that his wife had died during childbirth just before their son, Afamefuna, was born. The fight came to an abrupt end without a winner.

It was later rumoured that on the day Igwebuike lost his wife but gained a son, Omasirichi stole to his ulo that night to console him, imploring him to forget about her and raise his son. Whatever happened that night between them was uncertain – howbeit Omasirichi swore nothing out of the ordinary happened, still Nwokeoma felt dishonoured.

Two weeks after the loss of his wife and the birth of his son, Igwebuike went hunting. His unfortunate woes began that day when he killed an eke, the smallest python in Aro, with his spear, which he claimed was intended for an antelope that escaped. Even though the python was not big, his action drew the ire of Aro, and he was pronounced an osu as tradition demands. In one fell swoop, Igwebuike moved from being Aro's strongest man and best hunter to an outcast who was forced to live in the outlying community, ignored, inadequate and forgotten.

'Please,' Ugommaeze whispered beneath her breath. 'For your sake please still be there.'

Ugommaeze came to a stop, looked around in a wary fashion, and when she was sure no one was walking behind or in front of her, she turned the corner into a pathway enclosed by strips of maize on both sides. She slowed her feet, looking closely ahead in hopes of sighting Afamefuna beneath the only tree that stood amidst the large piece of abandoned maize land. She stopped beneath the tree and swivelled, but he was nowhere in sight. Her shoulders fell knowing there was only one thing left to do; return back home. She heaved a depressed sigh and was about to walk away when she heard a noise behind her. She turned swiftly but there was nothing. She stood still swallowing her saliva and winced because it tasted bitter from fear.

'Who is there?' she raised her voice.

Villagers no longer frequented the maize land because it was rumoured that the maize crops might have been planted by an osu who was a farmer in a nearby village. No one associated with an osu or wanted anything attributed to them. If the word osu was attached to any rumour – however true or untrue the rumours might be – it marked the beginning of the end of that thing or person.

The wind became still, and at once became so furious again that the leaves on the tree began to dance and make strange sounds.

Ugommaeze made to take to her heels when a hand grabbed her from behind and she screamed. Then came loud laughter and she stopped screaming. She swivelled and saw it was Afamefuna laughing. She frowned and slapped him on his stomach. He laughed harder.

'Ouch!' He held his stomach.

'How could you scare me like that knowing it is almost dark?'

'That was for keeping me waiting for more than an hour.'

Ugommaeze wore a sorry face and leaned towards Afamefuna.

'I am sorry. I had a heart-to-heart with my Nna.'

Afamefuna opened his arms and she slid into his warm embrace.

'I am sorry about earlier.' Ugommaeze broke free from his embrace.

'It wasn't your fault. I knew he would pounce on me. To be fair, my father would react the same if it were the other way around. The other day, he warned that if he ever saw you in his compound, for every time he intended to strike you, he would strike me instead.'

They both laughed.

'It is not fair that we are made to suffer from a past that we knew nothing about.'

'Nothing in life is fair.' Afamefuna replied in a defeated tone.

Ugommaeze held onto him. 'Promise me you will never give up on us.'

'I promise.'

'Life is nothing if you do not fight for what you believe in, and I believe in us.'

Afamefuna stroked her face with gentle brushes. Silence fell on them.

'You are in danger,' Ugommaeze forced herself to say. 'When I tried to defend you, my Nna became possessed with the idea that you killed Chijioke.'

'Did he now?' Afamefuna asked, unfazed.

'He claims your father could not kill him, so he used you to end my father's lineage.'

'That is a heavy accusation.' Afamefuna pulled back in impulsive reflection. He shifted his gaze from her into the open air.

'Please forgive me. I meant to portray you in a good light, but he still found a way to fault your kindness.'

'It is not you, Ugommaeze. It is every other thing but us.'

Afamefuna let out a faint smile and stroked her cheek. 'But what if fate does not favour our love? What if our stars crossed long before we were born?'

'We are not star-crossed,' Ugommaeze rebuked him.

'But we are born from one,' he bit back. 'Your mother. My father. They failed. My father was branded an *osu*, and I the offspring of an *osu*.'

'But nobody dares to call him an *osu*.'

'Only from fear. Doesn't mean we're not treated as *osu*, or that they do not whisper it behind the walls of their *ulo*.'

Ugommaeze moved back in despair, her stomach trembled, with tears threatening in her eyes. She almost fell but for her hand that leaned against the tree. Afamefuna's warm hands came upon her shoulder and she felt safe again. In that instant, she knew nothing in the world mattered if she couldn't spend it with the man she loved. Even death wouldn't put them apart.

'My love,' Afamefuna began, 'I know—'

'I have a solution,' Ugommaeze interjected.

'Okay—'

'Let me carry your child. Neither my Nna nor fate can come between us when that happens,' she sounded certain.

'I won't want it any other way, but what you ask is—'

'I do not care,' Ugommaeze countered. 'I care about us, and the future we will build.'

Afamefuna let out a wide cheerful smile, gently stroking her cheek as he cast a long, tempting gaze into her eyes.

'Why do you smile?' asked Ugommaeze.

'Because I love to hear you speak, for music has not a far more pleasing sound than you.'

'You flatter me.'

'If truth is what you call flattery, then I do.'

Ugommaeze brushed her hands against the hair on his chest, grabbed his face in a gentle fashion and drew him in for a kiss. She pulled back, stared at him and wondered if they both wanted the same thing. She got the answer when he leaned forward to return the kiss, then pulled away, both eyes glued to hers. Afamefuna unfastened the brown loins-cloth round his waist all without taking his eyes off her. She gulped at the sight of his manhood. Ugommaeze made to take off the beads around her neck, but he stepped forward, took them from her hand and hung them on a branch of the tree.

Ugommaeze touched the bead around her waist.

'What about my waist beads?' asked Ugommaeze in an uneven, sensual tone.

'I like them.'

Their breath was now rapid and wanting, but Afamefuna wasn't in a hurry to loosen her wrapper.

He ran his hands up her body, bit by bit unwinding the loose cloth around her chest and her breasts came into full view. For the first time, he shifted his gaze from her eyes to her chest taking in the view of her well-rounded breasts which stared back at him upright. He placed one hand on her left breast and she let out a low moan. He leaned down towards her and with the support of his other hand directed her right breast into his lusty mouth, gritted his teeth lightly and tickled her nipples. Ugommaeze held him tight and in the twinkle of an eye got lost inside his masculinity.

'Cock-a-doodle-doo!'

The cry of cockerels in repetitive progression defiled the morning serenity of Aro. Ugommaeze blinked open her eyes, and the rising sun shone through the sky. She looked over at Afamefuna who was half asleep, his hands across her chest, and noticed a small pile of broken wood in smoke beside them. She smiled.

'Did you enjoy your night?' Afamefuna asked from his sleep. He slowly opened his eyes and a wide grin covered his face.

'The best I ever had. When did you make the fire?'

Afamefuna opened his eyes slowly, looked at spot and made a low guttural sound. 'In the middle of the night. I barely remember anything, except you and last night.'

They kissed. Slowly. And when they pulled away, the sound of their lips parting was elastic.

'Good morning,' he greeted, and she stroked a finger against his nose.

'I have to leave before it is discovered I didn't sleep at home.' Ugommaeze rose.

Afamefuna let out a smile, and watched her dress against the sun rising above her head.

'I am tempted to ask you to stay a bit. But as I am in danger already it would be foolish of me to light the flames which will set me ablaze.'

'I thought you laughed in the face of danger,' Ugommaeze teased. 'It is one of the things I find attractive about you.'

'The fear of your father is the beginning of wisdom,' Afamefuna mocked.

'You can say that again.'

Ugommaeze grabbed her beads from the tree branch and was about to put them on when Afamefuna offered to help her. She bent her neck as he slipped them on, and his mind was at once transported to last night when he had slipped into her confines and unleashed his virility back and forth inside her.

They held hands as they set forth out of the maize farm in silence, for neither of them knew what fate had in store for them. The one thing they knew and agreed upon was that whatever it was, their love so strong would repulse and rewrite their destinies.

'Wait!' Afamefuna stopped and prevented Ugommaeze from moving forward. 'Do you hear that?' he said, swivelling around.

They stood at a clearing which led to four different paths.

'What is it?' Ugommaeze followed his eyes with a worried look. Afamefuna leaned his ear forward.

'I hear many footsteps matching towards us.' He shut his eyes and listened closer. 'I think it is a mob.'

Ugommaeze made an attempt to shout but he covered her mouth. She spun round, poised to run.

'They must have found us through the smoke,' Afamefuna said in a regretful tone. He looked at Ugommaeze. 'It is too late to run.'

'No, we can still run.'

'I would rather stand in the face of danger than run. If I run now, I will run forever.'

Tears threatened Ugommaeze's face. From the first day her and Afamefuna's legs had crossed paths in the bush – after she stumbled upon him and Chijioke returning from a hunting trip – she felt in the marrow of her bones their inevitable end with the brush of their lips. She often cried at night wondering why her heart had given in to a man whose father was an enemy to her father, yet, she couldn't fault fate for their paths crossing as theirs was love at first sight, a forbidden fruit which tasted so sweet. Who had ever loved, that hadn't loved at first sight?

'This is where we say our goodbyes.' Afamefuna rubbed his hands against her cheeks.

'No,' Ugommaeze broke down in tears, 'I will not say goodbye. Goodbye means going away and going away means forgetting you. So no, Afamefuna, I will not say goodbye, we will stay together until the very end.'

They broke down in tears and held each other in a tight embrace. There was nothing more left to say, they were at a point where words no longer had eloquence.

The mob – including a few warriors – came into view, led by

Nwokeoma, the high Chief and a few village elders. Afamefuna didn't pay them any attention even as their roars drowned the air; he heard only the beating heart of the woman in his arms. The angry mob stopped and Nwokeoma stepped forward.

'You killed my son, and now you dare kidnap my daughter!' shouted Nwokeoma. 'Step away from her this very minute.'

Afamefuna for the first time turned to face Nwokeoma and the mob behind him who wielded sticks and stones.

'Nna,' Ugommaeze cried out. 'He did not kidnap me.'

'Shut your mouth,' Nwokeoma snapped. He swivelled to the elders and said, 'He has poisoned her so deep that she defends him even when he does wrong. Yesterday, after the burial, she spoke ill of her late brother in order to defend this fool.' A quiet whisper ran through the mob. They went silent when Nwokeoma continued. 'I do not blame her; she is a woman after all, easily swayed by flatteries.'

'Nna,' Ugommaeze cried. 'I told no lies.'

'I am not surprised. You take after your mother,' replied Nwokeoma with melancholy.

The high Chief stepped forward, and placed a hand on Nwokeoma's shoulder. 'Afamefuna,' he called in an imposing tone. 'You're an osu whom the gods have rejected. You let your jealousy drive you to kill the son of a freeborn, and now you have kidnapped the daughter as well. The people reject you. The gods reject you. We have decided your fate.'

There was a roar from the mob, their sticks and metals clanging against each other.

The high Chief swivelled to the mob and motioned for calm.

'For the sins of Afamefuna,' the high Chief lifted his voice to the hearing of the mob, 'what punishment does he deserve? Death by the rope or banishment?'

'Death by rope! The rope! Kill him! Death by the rope!' the throng roared.

Afamefuna heaved a heavy sigh and shifted his gaze to Nwokeoma unfazed.

'Bring her over here!' Nwokeoma ordered two burly village warriors. They dropped their sticks and hurried towards Ugommaeze, a bit conscious not to touch Afamefuna, who didn't budge.

'No, please,' Ugommaeze fell on her knees, and they dragged her.

'Biko! Please!' Omasirichi shouted from behind, as she made her way through the mob. 'Nwokeoma, biko, for the love of me, spare the boy's life.'

Nwokeoma hissed and shoved Omasirichi to the ground. Ugommaeze rushed to her Nne's aid.

'Perhaps we are too hasty to pronounce judgement on Afamefuna,' an elder whispered to Nwokeoma. 'Let him have a fair trial to deny these accusations.'

'The voice of one man, over the voice of the people. That is not our culture.' Nwokeoma flashed the elder a mild frown.

'Kill him! Kill him! The rope!' chanted the mob with renewed vigour. Nwokeoma let out a proud grin and lifted his fist. There was silence. 'We shall hear the high Chief give his final judgement,' he said.

'Afamefuna,' the high Chief began, 'you are guilty of these crimes as accused, and for your crimes you shall hang to death.'

'Yeeeaaaa!' the mob erupted into loud celebration. On the backdrop of the celebration, Nwokeoma and Afamefuna exchanged daring glances with each other, both poised and ready to pounce on the other should the need arise.

Nwokeoma motioned to the crowd to stop, then motioned two warriors to grab Afamefuna. The warriors wore delight on their face, honoured to have been chosen to capture Afamefuna.

Afamefuna didn't flinch as the warriors approached him, crouched, each looking ready to grab him. The first warrior stretched his hand to grab Afamefuna, Afamefuna dodged him with ease, circling both warriors and studying their feet. The warrior made another attempt to grab Afamefuna, and this time, Afamefuna dodged him and struck a punch into the warrior's bare chest, grabbed his hand and flung him to the ground. The other warrior took two quick steps backward and the cheering mob went silent.

'You wish to hang me for crimes I did not commit,' Afamefuna flashed Nwokeoma a stern gaze, 'and yet, you come to me with sticks and stones!?' he chuckled. 'You seem to forget who I am and what I am made of.' His voice echoed in their silence as the terror on their faces made him grin.

'Here I am,' Afamefuna opened his arms. 'I dare you to arrest me. Send as many men as you can.'

'Pride courses through your veins just like your father,' Nwokeoma mocked. 'Your end shall be worse than his.' He turned to the mob and with a stern voice bawled, 'Twenty cowries to the man who brings Afamefuna to his knees.'

The mob murmured among themselves, contemplating who should go first. A warrior beat his chest and marched forward amidst the invigorating cheers from the mob. As he got closer to Afamefuna, he counted his steps. He had barely made a stance before Afamefuna grabbed, lifted him from the ground up and punched him so hard that what followed was a loud gasp from the mob which quelled the cheers.

Nwokeoma scowled. He motioned to a mobster to match up to Afamefuna. Petrified, the mobster lifted his stick and ran towards Afamefuna, yelling.

Afamefuna knocked him to the ground with ease.

Nwokeoma fumed, his breath becoming rapid with impatience. He motioned to a warrior to grab Afamefuna. The warrior approached with feigned audaciousness, but no one cheered. Face to face, they locked hands and struggled to take each other down for a few seconds to the growing delight of the mob and Nwokeoma. A few seconds later, Afamefuna hit the warrior on his knee and broke his bone.

The warrior wailed. Nwokeoma scowled. Ugommaeze and Omasirichi hid their smiles.

Afamefuna, now breathing fast, shouted, 'Is there no one else? Is that all you've got?'

Nwokeoma folded his fist and stepped forward cracking his neck. Afamefuna stepped back in awe, looked at Ugommaeze, then back to Nwokeoma.

'You are a fool not to have run when you had the chance,' Nwokeoma said.

'Cowards die many times before their fall,' replied Afamefuna. 'I am no coward.'

'Yes. But you are the son of your father. And you are a fool.'

'Nwokeoma, I will not fight you.'

'Then you are a bigger fool.'

Nwokeoma threw himself into the air and swung a vicious punch at Afamefuna.

Afamefuna fell.

* * * *

Ugommaeze couldn't and didn't stop running, because any minute she dared to pause to catch her breath could mean death for Afamefuna. She ran like his life depended on her; it actually did. It never occurred to her until now how long the distance from the village centre to the periphery of Aro was, because for the times she had undertaken such a journey, she was accompanied by Afamefuna under the influence of love. Love perhaps made short the distance in those moments, but today was not a journey for love, it was a journey for survival, a journey for life and death, and she didn't care how the long the distance was to find the only man who was feared and strong enough to fight off her Nna and the entire village – Igwebuike.

Ugommaeze wondered what Igwebuike's reaction would be on seeing her, having warned she should never set foot in his compound; she was, however, confident that he was a proper Igbo man who wouldn't strike a woman, no more the daughter of the woman his heart still beat for in secret. She thought about how life had been unfair to Igwebuike and how he had been treated by the people that claimed they loved him. What worried her more was that the same people who roared and cheered Igwebuike when he was the village champion, were the same people who now roared and cheered her father in his misdeeds. If there was anything to learn in Igwebuike's fall it was that the glory one holds today often fades when the morrow dawns. Even with Igwebuike's descent from fame to shame, Afamefuna told her his father would often claim not to hate the people of Aro regardless of how they treated him. He believed that while love blinds, hate plucks the eye. At first when he was cast out, he hated everyone and everything, then it occurred to him that he was hating people who themselves didn't realise he hated them; in the end, his mental state was in disarray while they walked about free.

'It is foolish to hate,' Afamefuna told her Igwebuike often said. Ugommaeze thought the man in his saying was wise, and that her Nna, if the case were reversed, would have been the opposite.

Ugommaeze burst into the compound and met Igwebuike sharpening his machete. She fell on her knee and broke into tears.

'Afamefuna is about to be hanged this very minute; he is accused of killing Chijioke,' she cried.

Igwebuike rose at once, his machete shining in front of Ugommaeze. He looked at her closely with an inscrutable gaze, and Ugommaeze wondered if he was trying to make certain she spoke the truth. The coarse beard which covered his face made it difficult to tell. It was by the tone of his voice she knew he had become angry.

'Where?'

'The village square.'

He turned and grabbed his skin-bag.

'And your mother?'

'She weeps and begs.'

Igwebuike ran, and Ugommaeze ran after him.

* * * *

Over the *Erigheri* tree hung a strong brown rope which sat around Afamefuna's neck. He kept still and without expression, waiting for the moment the elders would decide among themselves who would remove the lump of wood from under his feet and end him. No one wanted to be the one to strike the final blow and incur the wrath of Igwebuike. Nwokeoma was eager, but it was not his place to take such action except on the instruction of an elder.

Afamefuna looked up again, and there was no sight of Ugommaeze. He let out an aching sigh then looked piteously at the throng of villagers who gathered around the village square hungry to see an innocent man hang for a crime he didn't commit. They walked in misguided hate only because they were led by one.

'Nwokeoma!!' a voice roared from behind the throng. 'Nwokeoma!' the voice echoed again, this time more furious than the first. The crowd swivelled to see who roared in such anger. It was Igwebuike. Slowly, they began to give way for him as he made his way to the tree while they clutched one another and whispered in inaudible chatter.

Nwokeoma hurried to Afamefuna and kicked the lump of wood to the ground. Afamefuna strangled in silence as he swung from side to side.

Ugommaeze ran to hold Afamefuna from swinging.

'Let him go or I will strike you in the face,' Nwokeoma warned his daughter.

'You will kill me too,' Ugommaeze retorted, struggling to hold Afamefuna still.

Nwokeoma fumed, contemplating his next action, when Igwebuike came up behind him. The men stood face to face.

'I would only ask once. Cut my son loose,' Igwebuike ordered.

'Over my dead body,' Nwokeoma replied and folded his fist.

'Then so shall it be.'

'You are an *osu* and should not—'

Igwebuike attacked Nwokeoma with his machete, swinging twice against him, but Nwokeoma was swift to dodge both strikes, howbeit the last swing left a small cut on his skin. Everyone gasped. Omasirichi covered her mouth in shock.

Nwokeoma looked at the cut, winced and looked back at Igwebuike.

'You swing against a defenceless man.'

Igwebuike threw his machete to the side without shifting his furious gaze from Nwokeoma. There was a resolve in his eyes; only one of them would walk out of the fight alive, and it would not be Nwokeoma.

Nwokeoma threw a punch which smashed into Igwebuike's face, then he immediately made to lift and throw him down but Igwebuike escaped his grip. Igwebuike spat blood and a tooth fell out.

Igwebuike folded his fist, crouched and motioned his opponent towards him. They slapped each other's hand, waiting, patient for who would slip so the other could take advantage and strike. Exasperated, Nwokeoma grabbed Igwebuike in an attempt to throw him down but Igwebuike stood firm. Igwebuike countered by moving slightly to the left, stretched out his hand and grabbed Nwokeoma from behind the head, and with his face now parallel, he slammed Nwokeoma's face to the ground. There was a loud pant from the crowd. Igwebuike then turned Nwokeoma on his back and sat over him.

'First you took the woman I love,' Igwebuike punched Nwokeoma. 'Then you took my respect,' he swung another punch hard into Nwokeoma's face. 'Now you want to take my son too!?' Igwebuike's fist was about coming down on Nwokeoma again when Omasirichi hurried onto her knees before him.

'Igwe, please. He is still my husband.'

Igwebuike stopped his fist in front of Nwokeoma's nose. He looked up at Omasirichi, both gazing at the other with unspoken emotions. He knew she still loved him because she had called him by the name she called him when their love was in its prime. He slowly attempted to touch her but she moved away. He shifted his gaze to Nwokeoma on the ground, and spat at his side. He stood and made for Afamefuna when Nwokeoma rose from behind and attempted to hit him with a wood he had picked up from the floor but Igwebuike swivelled just in time to grab him and throw him to the ground.

'I should kill you,' Igwebuike threatened him with his hand squeezing Nwokeoma's throat.

'And risk losing everything?' Nwokeoma struggled to say.

Igwebuike casted a glance at Omasirichi, who stared them in ambivalence. 'You already took everything from me.'

Bit by bit, Igwebuike's grip became firmer around Nwokeoma's neck.

'Everybody, on your knees,' came a strange voice from behind, and then a gunshot followed.

They all ducked and looked behind them towards the voice. They were surrounded by a number of white men with fancy rounded-sticks, and the man who led them carried a firearm which looked more advanced than their Egbe. Among the white men stood an

Igbo man whom they all recognised – Nwankpa. He was a native of Aro and an osu, who, like Igwebuike, had been cast out of the village. He had remained on the periphery of Aro for a while but then was seen no more. The last that was heard of him were rumours that he went about in search of white men to learn how to speak English with a promise to exact revenge on the village that had cast him out. Nwankpa had fulfilled that promise.

The leader of the white man aimed his gun at Afamefuna and fired. The rope around Afamefuna's neck loosed and he fell to the ground, coughing.

As Ugommaeze lay on the ground, she saw that her mother was the only villager standing and she looked in pain. Omasirichi coughed blood and fell with a thud.

'Nne!' Ugommaeze shouted and ran to her mother.

Nwokeoma and Igwebuike ran after her. They knelt before Omasirichi.

'Stay where you are,' the white man with the gun shouted.

Afamefuna lay poised and ready to pounce on the white man pointing his gun at Ugommaeze.

'Nne,' Ugommaeze cried, 'please don't die.'

Omasirichi strained her eyes to see her daughter, her husband, and the man whom she truly loved all by her side. She forced a loving smile at them then lifted her feeble hand to fondle Igwebuike but it fell lifeless before she could reach his face. Igwebuike grabbed her hands to his face, closed his eyes and wept. When he opened his eyes, they were red.

Igwebuike grabbed the handle of his machete buried in the sand, and made a slight nod at Afamefuna. Afamefuna picked a stone and threw it at the white man with the gun, and in that moment of distraction, Igwebuike flung his machete into the man.

Igwebuike ran after the white man and just as he fell to the ground, he dragged the machete out of his chest and threw it into the back of another white man attempting to run away. He then grabbed a white man when another hit him with his stick from behind. Igwebuike dropped him, turning to the man who had hit him, and the man trembled. Igwebuike grabbed the man and was about to snap his neck when the one he had freed picked up the gun and shot into the air.

Igwebuike paused and looked at the man who had fired; the gun was pointed at Ugommaeze. He let go of the man and surrendered.

'Round them up,' the white man said. He walked up to Igwebuike. 'Your value just went up.' He hit Igwebuike with the back of the gun

* * * *

Ugommaeze opened her eyes and found her hands and feet were in chains; there were other women in chains too, a few she knew from Aro, others she didn't.

'Where is this place?' she thought out loud.

'Ugommaeze,' she heard Afamefuna's muffled voice call.

'Afamefuna,' she called, swivelling to where his voice came from.

'Look down, there is a hole.'

Ugommaeze looked at the bottom of the divide which separated where she and Afamefuna were and saw the hole. She peered in and could only see Afamefuna's eye. They attempted to touch each other but the chains around their hands prevented them.

'Where are we?' Ugommaeze asked.

'We are on a big boat they call the *Morovia*. We have been captured as slaves,' said Afamefuna miserably.

'Slaves! What about my Nna and—'

'We are all here, along with some strange people. I think they were captured from a different place.'

'Where are we going?'

'I do not know, but it cannot be anywhere good. Save your strength, you will need it.'

Afamefuna sat up against the wooden divide. The vessel tumbled and they smash their heads against the dirty beams.

There was a loud moan from the slaves. Igwebuike, bloody, was chained to a corner, but he didn't moan. He wore a despondent look; he cared about nothing.

"I would kill Nwankpa if I get a hold of him,' Nwokeoma boasted.

Igwebuike tilted his head slowly towards Nwokeoma. He scoffed, 'You feed your pride rather than mourn the loss of your wife?' but Igwebuike wasn't asking, he was perplexed.

'What good is me mourning the dead when I am in chains?' Nwokeoma replied with a frown. 'Let the dead bury the dead.'

Igwebuike shook his head. 'And you wonder why she gave you her hand, but gave me her heart.'

Nwokeoma, charged with fury, attempted to raise his fist at Igwebuike, but for the chains around his wrist that prevented him. 'You owe your life to these chains.'

Igwebuike flashed him an unfazed mocking gaze and returned to his solitude. He mumbled a prayer in Igbo and then returned his gaze to Nwokeoma, who was still staring at him in fury.

'How does it feel' Igwebuike asked, 'to be a slave? To be an outcast beyond Aro and beyond the seas?'

Nwokeoma's fury abated. He looked at the men around him, all in chains and helpless.

'Now you know how I felt all those years Aro branded me an *osu* even without chains.'

Nwokeoma sat back in silence.

'Afamefuna,' Ugommaeze called, tapping her chain against the divide between them. 'Is there a way we can get out of here?

'No,' Afamefuna responded in a defeated voice.

The door swung open and a ray of light covered a section of the dark room. Nwankpa walked in with wary steps. He looked behind him, but there was no one, and he shut the door behind him.

'A man who sells his people to foreigners for money,' Nwokeoma spat.

'There is no difference between me, the high Chief and the elders of Aro who label their own people *osu*. The weak ones you sell as slaves for money in the guise of punishment and economic development,' Nwankpa countered. He turned to Igwebuike and Afamefuna. 'You must understand me better.'

'When you choose to forgive those who hurt you, you take away their power. That is what you should have done,' Igwebuike told him.

'You only say that because you were not sold,' Nwankpa replied. 'You do not know what it means to be born a free man, but branded an *osu* and sold into slavery. I am no longer bound in chains because I am smart.'

'We are all slaves to someone or something,' Afamefuna said in low tone. 'Freedom is an illusion.'

Afamefuna's response brought with it a silence which reeked of sudden realisation.

The door to the section where Ugommaeze was chained swung open, then came footsteps which stopped and Ugommaeze began to scream. Afamefuna tried to struggle out of his chains in a futile attempt to save her. Her scream faded when the door banged against its lock, and in no time, her cry was silenced by the slapping of the sea against the ship.

'What is happening?' Afamefuna stood to Nwankpa, furious. 'Where are they taking her to?' he barked.

Nwankpa motioned him to be quiet.

'She will be the Captain's sex slave until he is done with her and requests another slave,' Nwankpa answered.

Afamefuna struggled to break himself free, and again, his attempt was futile. He panted urgently.

'I stole the key to your chains,' continued Nwankpa, not minding Afamefuna's theatrics. 'I can take you to where she will be.'

'Why should I believe you want to help me? You did this to us after all.'

Nwankpa heaved a sigh, followed by silence.

Igwebuike looked up closely at Nwankpa.

'Because now he realizes the freedom they promised him for when we arrive *obodo-oyibo* is a hoax.' Igwebuike scoffed. 'Freedom is indeed an illusion.'

'I admit I did a wrong, but I want to correct it,' Nwankpa broke his reflective silence.

'Which is a good thing,' Igwebuike said, then flashed Nwokeoma a look of disdain, 'unlike some.'

Nwankpa crouched, gathered sand and drew a location map with his fingers.

'This is where she will be,' he said pointing at a block at the end of the map, 'the Captain's sex lair.'

Afamefuna bent and studied the map. He focused on it like it was a matter of life or death. A few seconds later, he stretched his chained hand to Nwankpa who unlocked the chains on his hands and feet.

'Set the rest free, and kill any white man in your path.'

Afamefuna started for the exit.

'Where are you headed?' Igwebuike asked him.

'To introduce myself to the captain.'

At that, Afamefuna hurried to the door, looked both ways, then crept away.

Nwankpa set Igwebuike free and went about setting the other slaves free. He got to Nwokeoma and cast a long look at him. 'If I set you free, would you do anything stupid?'

'You betrayed your clan, and you think I will forgive you because you decided to have a change of heart?' Nwokeoma scowled. 'I do not promise I won't break your neck.'

Nwankpa winced and made to walk away.

'Set him free,' Igwebuike ordered Nwankpa.

'You heard him,' Nwankpa countered, 'he will break my neck.'

'He would do no such thing, I assure you.' Igwebuike turned to Nwokeoma and said, 'Save your strength for those who put us on this ship.'

'You cannot tell me what to do and what not to do,' barked Nwokeoma, 'you are an *osu*.'

Igwebuike smiled. 'Look around you. We are all outcasts, in case you haven't noticed.'

Nwokeoma looked around him. Staring back at him were faces of men in chains, battered and helpless.

Igwebuike motioned to Nwankpa to unlock the chain. Nwankpa hesitated, then went on to unlock the chain. He hurried off to unlock others.

The chain fell off a bald Black man with hostile scars on his face. He rubbed his wrist and inhaled freedom.

'Thank you for setting my people free,' the bald man said to Igwebuike.

'You should thank him,' Igwebuike replied the man. 'He is the one with the key.'

The man swivelled to Nwankpa and said, 'Thank you.'

'Your accent, you must be from the west?' ask Igwebuike.

'Togo to be precise. My people and I were gathered for our Voodoo festival when the whites attacked us.'

'Are they all your people?' Igwebuike looked around.

'My people are scattered around the ship. We met some when we were brought onboard, but now we are all one, and will fight as one.'

Igwebuike let out a grin and they shook hands firmly.

'Look at us,' said a voice from behind, 'we are weak, how can we fight people with guns?'

There was silence, each man looking at the other devoid of an answer.

'You think you are weak?' Igwebuike asked irritated. 'Do you really think you are weak?' he raised his voice. 'Look around. These white men wielding guns didn't capture us because we are weak, they need our strength to work on their plantations, they enslave and put us in chains because we are strong. Now, do not think you are weak because you are no warrior – if life has taught me anything, it is that the weak can overcome if the weak persist. Henceforth, think not yourselves as weak, for you are Black, and Black is strong.'

The freed slaves clapped their fists against their palms, making a muffled cheer.

'Go around the ship and set free as many captives you can find,' Igwebuike said to Nwankpa.

Nwankpa nodded and left with two men behind him.

To the others Igwebuike said, 'It is time for us to unleash chaos. Freedom isn't given, it is fought for.'

At that, Igwebuike marched out and others followed behind him. Nwokeoma watched as the slaves hurried away, feeling alive. He stood back in uncertainty.

On hearing sailors and crew chatter in their twisted tongues, Afamefuna came to a stop and hid behind the steps which led to the upper deck. A white sailor climbed down and motioned his fellows to hurry down. Afamefuna watched them open a hull below deck and just as he made to creep away, the sailor and his fellows returned carrying a dead slave and threw him overboard. Afamefuna couldn't make out what they said as they headed back up, but their mocking laughter gave him an idea. He was enraged all over again.

When the coast was clear of white fellows, Afamefuna tiptoed to a level up the stairs and peered around the deck. With no one looking in his direction, he swiftly snuck into a storage room but froze on seeing a sailor just ahead of him behind some grain, which Afamefuna assumed was the sailor's duty to protect. Afamefuna took a closer look and saw the sailor was asleep. He let out a silent sigh of relief and carefully tiptoed his way into the cabin located at the end of the map Nwankpa had drawn him. He opened the door, and to his dismay and delight, Ugommaeze was at the end of the cubicle on her hands and knees, chained to the floorboards like the goats in Aro.

Afamefuna's heart leaped for joy, but he didn't notice a white fellow waxing his belt in the corner, and ran to embrace Ugommaeze.

The white man turned and his eyes met with the intruder. Before he could reach for his gun, Afamefuna jumped on him and twisted his neck until he was dead.

'Ugommaeze!' Afamefuna called.

'Afamefuna! Is that you?'

He ran to her in tears and embraced her; she cried too.

'I have never been so happy to see you.'

'Me too. I am sorry I couldn't do something to prevent this from happening,' he held her closely.

'But you can prevent what he said will happen next. Please get me out of these chains,' Ugommaeze cried.

'There is nothing to fear, I have already killed their captain.'

Ugommaeze looked at the lifeless body on the floor and shook her head. Afamefuna was about to respond when the door swung open. Afamefuna recognize the captain as the man who pointed a gun at Ugommaeze in the village square. He dived into a corner.

The captain walked in holding a bottle of whisky to his chest; he was drunk. He muttered gibberish and slammed the bottle on the table, spilling whisky over the smooth mahogany surface. He was about to sit when he saw Ugommaeze bent and ready to be taken. He let out a lecherous grin and started towards her.

'Missed me?' the captain flashed his teeth and Ugommaeze flinched, he reeked of alcohol. He placed his hand on her back and moved it down her waist. Ugommaeze shook persistently.

'Feisty! I like it.'

The captain smacked her buttocks with delight, flipped up her wrapper to expose them, and rubbed them gently. Ugommaeze sobbed.

In the corner, Afamefuna raged. He rose silently, folding his fist contemplating when to strike, and he slipped over a spill of water. He was quick to find his footing; he was, however, not quick enough because the captain at once swivelled in the direction of the noise.

'Who is there!?'

It was then he noticed the white fellow lifeless on the ground. In one quick leap he reached to grab his gun from behind his desk, but Afamefuna came out of hiding, pounced on him and swung a punch to the captain's face. Instead of landing on the floor, the captain put out his hand to the desk to steady himself and pushed back towards Afamefuna while latching on to a table knife. Afamefuna hurriedly grabbed the gun the captain wanted to reach. He pointed it at the captain, who froze. Afamefuna shot at the captain but the gun jammed.

While Afamefuna struggled to cock the gun, the captain drove the knife into him and drew blood from his arm. Afamefuna let out a suppressed moan and let go of the gun. The captain grabbed it and pointed it at Afamefuna.

'You should think twice before you make another move.' The captain cocked the gun.

Afamefuna lifted his hands in surrender, and blood began to drip down his arm.

'Well, well, well, what do we have here? A runner.'

'Please, don't hurt him,' Ugommaeze wept.

The captain hit her shoulder with the butt of his gun and she cried out loud.

'Ugommaeze, hold your tears!' Afamefuna fumed. 'Never show weakness to your enemy.'

'I will do anything you want.' She ignored Afamefuna. 'Please don't hurt him.'

The captain switched his gaze from Afamefuna to Ugommaeze then let out a devilish grin. 'Ah! You broke free to rescue her. Well, well, well, onboard *Morovia* we have an African Romeo and Juliet,' he laughed again.

Afamefuna groaned beneath his breath, fuming.

'Careful, Romeo, do not provoke me.'

Afamefuna turned to Ugommaeze and she made a silent plea. He let go of his fist.

'Attaboy!' the captain chuckled.

'Here's what happens next. You will stand over there and watch me sport with Juliet over here, and when I am done, I will give her to my boys while I sport with you too,' he grinned. 'Do you have a problem with that?'

Afamefuna hesitated. The captain pointed his gun at Ugommaeze. Afamefuna made a forceful nod.

His gun pointed at Afamefuna, the captain caressed Ugommaeze's buttocks, and ran his fingers across her anus.

Ugommaeze shuddered.

Afamefuna closed his eyes in an effort to control his rage.

'Open your eyes, Romeo,' the captain ordered. Afamefuna obeyed. 'I have a feeling I am going to enjoy this one.'

The captain laughed at Afamefuna's displeasure. As he began to loosen his belt, the roars of an angry mob erupted, followed by cries for help.

'What the fuck is going—,' his sentence was cut short as the sound of a gunshot followed the uproar.

'Kill them all!' he heard his men shout. Sporadic gunshots followed. He began to fasten his belt hastily and Afamefuna seized the opportunity to charge at him. The Captain swivelled and fired an erratic shot at Afamefuna, but undeterred, Afamefuna charged on and struck the captain with a punch, sending him to the ground. Afamefuna fell on him and continued to punch him, yelling, 'Who is using who for sport now?'

'Afamefuna! Afamefuna!' Ugommaeze shouted until he stopped. 'He is dead.'

Afamefuna looked at the captain again; his face lay still in the pool of his own blood.

'Quick, get me out of this. You are bleeding.'

'I know. It is just a knife—' Afamefuna fell back down as soon as he attempted to stand. He looked down at his leg and blood was gushing out. The shot the captain had fired had pierced him just above his kneecap. He bit his teeth as he groaned.

'Find the key and unchain me so I can cover the wound before it gets infected.'

Afamefuna reached into the captain's pocket, took out the key and set Ugommaeze free.

She dived on Afamefuna as the chains fell off her, locking herself around his bloody hands in tears.

'You are free now, my love, you are free,' he told her. Then, 'Arrggh!' he groaned and held his leg. 'Check how deep it is,' Afamefuna motioned her.

Ugommaeze, irritated, dipped her little finger into his wound and he let out a muffled groan. Ugommaeze trembled and removed her finger at once.

'Sorry! Sorry!' Ugommaeze pleaded. 'The bullet lies deep,' she said looking around, 'we need to get it out of you.' Her sentence had barely ended when the cabin door swung open and a white man wielding a shotgun ran in shouting, 'Captain, help us.' He paused on seeing Afamefuna and Ugommaeze staring right at him and his captain dead on the floor in his own blood. He pointed his gun at them, about to shoot. Ugommaeze and Afamefuna exchanged one last glance and closed their eyes, their hands joined together.

BANG! A gun went off. A few seconds later, they touched themselves, stunned, and opened their eyes. The white man fell and revealed Igwebuike wielding a shotgun.

'You owe me two tubers of yam at the next new yam festival,' Igwebuike said with a straight face.

Ugommaeze and Afamefuna laughed. She helped Afamefuna up and they ran out. On the deck, the slaves rounded up the ship's crew members lucky enough not to have been shot, thrown into the sea or beaten to death. The unlucky ones lay lifeless, riddled with bullet holes.

Igwebuike turned to a group of dispirited-looking Togolese. He went to them and saw they circled around a lifeless body. He looked closer and saw it was the bald Black man who had been chained in the same room as him. The Togolese lifted the body up and they started away. Igwebuike closed his eyes and paid his respects.

Afamefuna leaped to his father.

'You knew him?'

'Briefly,' Igwebuike opened his eyes.

A large number of slaves rushed above the deck, and Nwankpa

and Nwokeoma came up behind them. Igbo kinsmen embraced each other, while other Africans searched about for familiar faces.

Ugommaeze was staring at the calmness and beauty of the sea when she heard someone called her name.

'Nna!' she turned at once and saw her father running towards her. They ran into each other's arms and embraced.

'Are you all right!? Were you hurt?'

'I am fine, Nna. I am just happy to see you.'

They locked in an embrace again.

'We should throw the whites into the sea and let the sharks feed on them,' said an Aro kinsman, furious.

'Then there is no difference between us and them,' Nwokeoma answered and turned to him.

'They stole us from our homes,' countered another kinsman, 'divided husbands from their wives, sons and daughters from their mothers, and mothers from their unborn generations.'

'Still, we are not savages like them,' Nwokeoma replied.

'They killed your wife, and that is all you would say?' the kinsman fired back.

'A man I know once said, when you choose to forgive those who hurt you, you take away their power.' Nwokeoma cast a glance at Igwebuike; there was an exchange of respect in their brief stare. 'What we should think about now is how to return back home.'

'It is already too late,' said Ugommaeze staring into the sea. Others turned towards her and followed her eyes; in the distance ahead of them was dry land.

The people began to murmur in fright. Nwankpa looked far into the land and closed his eyes against the buffeting waters of the sea. He opened his eyes with a sense of guilt, watching his people murmur, then he stepped back quietly and went below the deck.

'We should sail back before we reach their lands,' shouted another kinsman above the murmuring.

'We do not know the way back, and even if we did, they would send another ship to recapture us at sea,' replied Igwebuike.

'An *osu* has no right to speak when freeborn men make decisions,' replied the kinsman, furious.

'Look around you,' Afamefuna laughed. 'We are all outcast.'

They exchanged awkward glances with one another, surrounded by the broken silence of the sea.

'Igwebuike led the men that freed us from our captor, and he is the eldest amongst us,' Nwokeoma broke the silence. 'I vote he lead us into our next action as our high Chief.' He lifted his hand.

Except for a few, the majority of kinsmen lifted their hands in support. Ugommaeze lifted her hand, Afamefuna too.

'The yes is more than the no,' Nwokeoma put down his hand and turned to Igwebuike. 'This is not how you would have wanted to get back what is rightfully yours, but this is where we find ourselves.'

Igwebuike and Nwokeoma exchanged a fleeting look of respect, apology and acknowledgment. Nwokeoma then gave a slight nod and turned to his daughter. She flashed him a prideful glance.

'You are now the son of a high Chief,' Ugommaeze whispered to Afamefuna. They chuckled without a sound.

'High Chief,' called a troubled kinsman, 'what do we do now? We are far away from Aro and do not know the way back.'

'We should wait for when we land and beg the white men to send us back home,' said another.

Igwebuike cleared his throat. 'The white man can steal us from our homes, they can put us in chains, they can flog and starve us, but they cannot take away our pride. We are Ndi Igbo; they cannot take our will. We may be hopeless, homeless, but when you beg a man for freedom, you will never be free.'

The people nodded in unison.

'So what do we do now?'

Igwebuike heaved a sigh and stared into the sea.

'I would rather die than be enslaved by those white baboons,' said Ugommaeze.

'Coming from a woman,' a voice from behind mocked and some laughed.

'I too would rather die,' said Afamefuna and the laughter waned. He flashed Ugommaeze a supportive glance.

Nwokeoma cast an unfathomable gaze at both lovers.

'We may be far from home,' said Igwebuike, 'but we are guided by the dead, the living and the unborn.'

Ugommaeze took Afamefuna aside and held him close. He was cold and in pain, and she knew he would never be warm again.

'I don't care what happens next,' whispered Ugommaeze to Afamefuna. 'All I care is that we are together.'

'It saddens me that this is how our love ends, in an unknown land trapped by water, instead of in our ulo with offspring to bear our names.'

Ugommaeze smiled. 'We may not have an ulo or offspring, but we have us.'

They touched foreheads then she slipped into his embrace. Over Afamefuna's shoulder, Ugommaeze looked below the deck and saw

Nwankpa had hanged himself, a chain and key in his hands. Suicide in Igbo was taboo, but she understood why he had done it, why he chose to leave this world a free man rather than be bound in chains again. He died with a smile on his face – a free man. In that moment Ugommaeze knew how she wanted to go, and knew the man she loved would choose to go the same way with her. Their decision would break her father's heart, but she didn't care, she would rather immortalise their love than leave to fate and tradition the demise of two star-crossed lovers.

'We have both chosen to drown,' announced Ugommaeze over the voices of arguing kinsmen. Silence fell upon the ship.

Afamefuna cast a long contemplative glance at her. He nodded slightly at her, held her hand. 'Yes.'

'The water spirit brought us here, the water spirit will take us back,' Igwebuike said and moved to join Afamefuna and Ugommaeze. 'That is how we choose to go.'

'This is nonsense,' barked a burly kinsman. 'I choose to stay and fight when we land,' he stepped back.

'I believe when we land, we can still beg them to send us back home,' one woman said and a few nodded in agreement. They joined the burly Igbo man.

Nwokeoma joined his daughter and she embraced him with delight. One man held his wife in an attempt to join Afamefuna, but the wife broke free from his grip. 'I am sorry,' she said, 'I don't want to die.' The man nodded and they went their separate ways. Ugommaeze, Afamefuna, Igwebuike, Nwokeoma and nine other kinsmen stood at the edge of the deck and watched their other kinsmen walk back, grabbing guns and any weapon they could find.

Ugommaeze looked up; the ship was fast approaching to the dry land. 'It is now or never,' she said and turned to Igwebuike. 'Lead us.'

The ship came to a stop. A signpost by the edge of the harbour read Dunbar Creek, St Simons Island; they were at Glynn county in Georgia. Igwebuike stood at the edge of the deck and began to sing in Ibo, 'The water spirit brought us here, the water spirit will take us home,' and the others joined him in singing. Nwokeoma joined him at the edge, they exchanged acknowledging glances and continued singing, the echoes of their voices louder as they repeated the notes.

Igwebuike jumped first, followed by Nwokeoma, and others followed, leaving Ugommaeze and Afamefuna holding hands. They exchanged one final loving gaze and she pulled in his lips with a deep kiss.

'Together forever.'

Afamefuna nodded. 'Together forever.'

They jumped holding hands, and formed a ring in the water.

The End

By the time bounty hunters dived in to recover the slaves. They met them in circles, holding hands, standing dead. Nwokeoma's hand was stretched to Igwebuike, both about to shake. Ugommaeze and Afamefuna were embracing.

The bounty hunters were paid $10 per head for the slaves they were able to rescue.

The actual number of deaths is uncertain as some bodies were never found.

The historic site is now known as Igbo Landing.

This later became known as the first march against slavery in America.

EVEN GODS CRY

Patience is most needed
In this world oft' hurrying near

- Albrin Junior

Everything had gone wrong since William turned twenty-five. The recurring voices in his head, the nightmares which echoed in his sleep, and the unknown pile of bodies soaked in an ocean coloured in blood. He could understand none of it, why they were beginning to steal the quiet hours of his night. The last nightmare did it for him. He saw the temperate but terrifying faces of three unknown women, witches, making mocking gestures at him. They didn't hurt him; rather, they loved him, beckoned him towards them.

William popped his eyes open and jumped out of bed so as not to be lured by the witches' gentle eyes, yet, when he sighed and turned to his side, he saw the same eyes lingering in the corner of his bedroom. He grabbed his shirt and ran out. He had had enough; he was going to tell his parents. As the only child, he was confident his parent would listen, they always did. He didn't always get what he wanted, but they made life comfortable for him, maybe too comfortable for his own good, but it was a privilege he enjoyed.

William's parents, Mr and Mrs Craig, sat on the couch in the parlour, a little more relaxed than usual, as they listened to their son narrate all his fears and dreams. They burst into laughter. William was stunned, unsure if they mocked him, or found the events of his nightmare impossible.

'Did I say something funny?' asked William.

'No, honey, you didn't,' his mother responded amidst her waning laughter.

'Then why are you laughing? I came to you for help,' retorted William in a disconcerted tone. His mother stopped laughing but not his father, who only stopped after his wife flashed him a warning look. He cleared his throat and said, 'Son, we are all ears.'

* * * *

'What nightmare have you been having?' asked Clara, William's longtime girlfriend.

William recoiled. Aside his parents, she was the next best thing to have happened to him. They talked about everything and anything, an inseparable pair, but since his nightmares had begun, he told her nothing. They were unsettling enough that it scared him; he didn't want to scare her too.

'My mum told you!?'

'She was worried. She wanted me to talk to you.'

'She shouldn't have told you,' he frowned, and turned his face aside. He couldn't shake away the feeling that there was something his parents were not telling him; it lurked behind the façade of their laughter, something near apprehension.

William had for the third time made love to Clara when his parents came to break the news that they would be going on a trip to South Africa to celebrate their 45th wedding anniversary. He wanted to be happy for them, he tried to be happy, but, for some reason which he couldn't fully understand, he was sad, and no, it wasn't because he was a selfish son, he found that with the news came an inkling – a feeling that he was unable to shake off – that things would go from bad to worse. Possibly beyond worse.

'You're not happy for us?' asked Mrs Craig.

'Yes. I mean no, I am happy. I am just wondering why now?'

'Your dad wanted to give me a different treat. It's our sapphire anniversary,' his mother responded.

'This is rubbish!' Mr Craig barked. 'So I now have to convince my son about a decision I made because he is from a woke generation!? Unbelievable.'

William flashed an apprehensive stare at his dad, a conservative African man unwilling to change with the times.

'I wasn't—' William didn't find the need to defend himself, not like it would matter. 'When do you plan to leave?'

'Tomorrow. Morning. And you're driving us to the airport,' said his father, and he left the room. His mother shrugged and followed her husband. William lay back, crushed.

* * * *

Dawn came running faster than usual; at least, that was what William thought as he drove his parents to the airport that morning. He wanted to wait there till their flight departed, but they urged him to return home. He couldn't understand why they tried to keep a distance from him since he had told them about his nightmares. He drove back home. He cast his mind away from his worries, and thought how being home alone meant he and Clara would have ample time to chase each other around the house naked beneath their shirts and end up having sex on the couch, then in the kitchen. The thoughts excited him. He was a street away from home when his phone rang. He picked up.

'Hello,' came a male voice from the other end of the phone. The person spoke in a solemn voice which became uneasy towards the end of his message. William became uneasy too.

'I don't understand what you're saying?' asked William in a stern shaky voice. 'What do you mean by an accident?'

The man on the phone paused; it was difficult for him to relate the news.

'I am calling from NL international airport where a Mr and Mrs Craig took a flight to South Africa. Our flight manifesto says you are their son. Is that right?'

'Yes.'

'Unfortunately, Mr William,' the man let out a momentary sigh then continued, 'their plane crashed a few minutes after it departed the airport.'

William shuddered. The phone fell. His world crashed. His undefined fear had become a reality. In his sadness, he drove to Clara's to seek solace. He met her door slightly open and walked in, too sad to hear the sounds of her moaning, nor did he notice the male clothes strewn around her living room. He opened the door to her bedroom. He saw Clara naked, having cowgirl sex with someone. For a short moment, the tears in his eyes dried. He moved closer in growing rage. He stopped when he saw the man she was riding. It was his best friend and his girlfriend entangled in the centuries-old battle of lovemaking. His rage died out. His world crashed a second time.

* * * *

William parked outside what used to be his parents' house. It had become tragic. Empty. Cold. Distant. Haunted with memories of what used to be.

He rented a self-contained room away from the city centre, far away from his former life. But though he moved as far away physically as possible, the memories and pain stuck with him like a twin. No sooner had he relocated than he heard that Clara had died. She had committed suicide because Jide, his used-to-be best friend, refused to take responsibility for her pregnancy. She died from shame and he felt no pity whatsoever. His anger wouldn't let him feel for a stranger – that was what she became in his eyes.

William started a new life and a new job as a waiter at a local restaurant, a restaurant he had stumbled upon by accident when he was stalking Aminat. On the morning he met her, he had gone to sleep the previous night in dire need of a distraction, something to make him forget where he was coming from, and forge a new path. It was his sixth month of mourning. The sun was barely up when he woke and went job hunting. It was then he saw Aminat, a dark, slim woman with captivating beauty, from across the road. He followed behind her, hoping for the right moment to approach her, to make her acquaintance. But the right moment didn't come, and he watched her, with disappointment, walk into a restaurant. He stood for a few seconds staring at the entrance of the restaurant, and only when he turned to leave did he see the '*Waiter wanted*' sign in the window. He walked in, and not only did he get the job, he got the girl.

It was a cold Saturday morning and William had had another nightmare, the first since he lost his parents. He sprung up.

'Are you okay?' Aminat asked as William tried to catch his breath. She stood and drew the curtains open. The rays of the sun shone in, and chased away the darkness in the room and in William's eyes. The faces of the three witches faded with the darkness.

'I am fine, dear,' he said in between breaths. 'Just a bad dream.'

Aminat rubbed his head, and continued dressing.

'Going somewhere?' asked William.

'Market. Remember?'

'Ah, yes. I didn't think it would be this early.'

'The earlier the better to avoid rowdiness.'

'Yeah, true.'

William lay back in bed, mulling over why his nightmares had returned after a long break. He thought he had left them behind in his past, and now that they were back in his present, he suddenly had a bad feeling about them.

'Walk me to the bus-stop,' said Aminat. 'I won't take long.'

William dragged himself out of bed, washed his faced and followed her to the bus-stop. He kissed her on the cheek and waved to her before she made to cross the road. She crossed the first lane and was about to cross the second when a red wagon jeep running out of control drove up behind her and knocked her off the ground. He hurried to the scene. The white shirt she wore was fast becoming red. People rushed to the scene, but the driver of the red wagon sped off. No one answered William's cry for help; instead, they stood in the distance capturing the pain of the scene with their phones. She died in his arms. The world heard him wail.

* * * *

There was a pattern, one he couldn't yet figure out. His nightmares were three women laughing and making fun of him, but whenever they weren't laughing and mocking him, they were smiling and beckoning him towards them. Whenever the latter happened, he woke only to soon lose someone he loved. It was the pattern with his parents and now Aminat.

Nights came and went, and William Craig barely slept. He feared to close his eyes because the images of him holding Aminat's lifeless body still haunted him. He feared that if he gave way to sleep, he would again be tortured by the image of the three witches laughing and mocking him. He found he had no reason to live, and because having no reasons to live gives reasons to die, he saw death as the next best option considering his reasons to live were dead. He had become a curse and didn't want to drown another soul in his grave pool.

William took out a piece of paper and a pen in an attempt to write a suicide note, but couldn't scribble a word. He knew of no one who loved him enough to read his note when he was gone. He drowned himself in three bottles of alcohol, then reached for the knife in the kitchen. He stared long at it, contemplating how to strike in himself a deep enough jab that wouldn't cause him pain, but nothing came to mind; his death would be fatal and slow. He made a sign of the cross, and whispered a prayer of forgiveness, but stopped halfway convinced that God hadn't heard any of his previous prayers, and was obviously not going to start now. He heaved a deep sigh, lifted the knife and was about to drive it into his palpitating heart, when as the knife came down, there was a loud knock on the door. A loud, repeated knock. He went to open it. It was his landlady. It was fate.

* * * *

William got another job which forced him to relocate to another apartment in the suburbs. His new job was engaging, working day and night as a fireman to quench fires, and deep down hoping the fires were his fears. His job made him too busy to be present in his life, so he didn't notice he had a new neighbour, Tracy Omolu. By the time they met, she had lived in the compound more than a month, but though he hadn't noticed her, she had noticed him. The first time they stumbled onto each other in the stairway, Tracy took the opportunity to introduce herself to William. She wore a bright smile, and her eyes were cheerful, and their hands, when they shook, were warm against each other's.

There was an exchange of sexual tension in their stare, and William, in an instant, felt uncomfortable. It was the first time in a long time he had been spellbound; he wanted to be happy again, wanted someone with an overflow of happiness to flood him, but he was afraid to dare to be happy.

'I hope this house isn't short of your expectations?,' asked William, breaking the tension in their gaze.

'Can one ever find a place that fits our wants?' Tracy teased.

William forced himself to laugh. What he really wanted to do was to run far away from her.

'Again, welcome,' he told her.

They exchanged one last flirtatious glance and went their ways. That night, he dreamt. He dreamt that Tracy walked into his room as he came out of the shower, naked, with his towel around his head. He told her to leave, but she refused, and in the heat of the moment, she grabbed his dick and kissed him long enough till he let himself relax. He grabbed her, pushed her back against the wall, and just as he made to tear her clothes off, a ghastly wind blew into the room. He turned to look at the window, and when he turned back to Tracy, she was gone. He moved back aghast, afraid and alarmed. He looked down and his towel was around his waist. The window banged against its frame and he shifted his gaze in that direction, petrified. The wind stopped. His father, covered in a white overall material was standing before him. The man stared at his son with a certain kind of fierceness.

'Dad! Is that… is that you!?'

'Don't drown another soul in your pool of death,' his father echoed.

'I don't understand!'

'No one lives and dies to himself.' His father's voice was stern and cold. 'You died the day you were born.'

'I died!?' William scoffed.

'Speak less and open your ears.'

'I am listening, Dad.'

'Then why mock me?'

* * * *

The story dates back to the late 1990s just before William was born. His parents had been married for ten years and without a child. His father was the son of a missionary who had come to dwell in Ogun state where he married his mother despite the disapproval of her parents. As time went on, his mother was faced with pressure, unable to bear to look over the fence without feeling ashamed of her childlessness. Each time she spoke to her husband about it, he always convinced her to let go off her worry and focus on serving God. His father's axiom to his mother used to be: 'A hunter's surest weapon is patience', to which she one day replied to him: 'A hunter with patience as his weapon is one day bound to be devoured by the same animal he patiently waits to kill.' His father spoke no more of patience after that. His father continued to live nobly and at peace with his situation – even though in secret he often worried about it, but his mother got worse, especially after her closest friend gave birth after eight years of barrenness. It was only then did his father realise that a man's goodness ends when a woman's pressure begins, as theirs was a kind of pressure to which all men, regardless of their nobility, were bound to fall prey. He fell.

Days later, they went into the forbidden forest to seek the three sisters' help – Fire, Wind and Rain. It wasn't as difficult as they had imagined. All his mother did was sleep outside the witches' hut, alone for two days. Nine months later, William Craig was born. All was looking fine for them until the incident on the night of the naming ceremony, which made them run away to Lagos, to start all over, away from the sisters so they wouldn't be able to take back the son they had given to them.

Twenty-five years later, the three witches appeared to his parents in a dream, informing them they had come take the son who had been given to them, but first, he would drown the souls of those he loved in his pool of death, beginning with them.

'No one live and dies to himself. You wanted a son, we gave you a god, he will bring death to everyone he loves,' Rain told them.

* * * *

Two weeks after William saw his father's ghost, he became more afraid of who he was, and in any way he could, he avoided bumping into Tracy. His plan failed one night as he arrived back from work and met Tracy standing by his door. William froze.

'You look surprised to see me,' said Tracy. William forced a smile. 'If I didn't know well, I would have thought you were avoiding me.'

'Why would I?' said William and he opened the door for them to enter.

Tracy made herself comfortable while William freshened up. When he returned to her, the scent that oozed off him made Tracy wanted to lick him. William sat down and Tracy closed the gap between them, then kissed him. He kissed back. He wanted to warn her to be wary of him, and a part of him tried to resist her covetous touch; he opened his mouth but the words wouldn't come out, instead, he was consumed by the softness of her lips, ensnared by her rhythmic moans. She pulled off his shirt and was reaching for his trousers, and he knew if she succeeded in touching his dick, there was no going back. William forced himself away from her.

'I am sorry.' He shied away from her. 'This can't happen.'

'Why?'

William thought for a few seconds then shook his head. 'This was a mistake, it shouldn't – it can't happen again.'

'What do you mean by mistake? Am I not good for you?' Tracy asked.

'I do not mean it that way. You are not the problem. I am.'

'William. Are you sure everything is okay?'

William raked his hand into his hair and nodded.

'When men say those words, the reverse is always the case.'

'The reverse is not the case here. You are the kind of woman any man would die for.'

'Except you.'

'What I am trying to say is that I'm not the kind of man you deserve. My life is a mess; anyone I love eventually dies.'

'Not anyone,' Tracy shot back. 'I will be the one who doesn't.'

Her words were followed by a long unhurried kiss. He wanted to tell her everything that had happened to those he loved, what his late father had told him about his birth, but couldn't bring himself to do it. He gave in to her without a fight, unbridled, allowing the beast in him to roam free in her.

* * * *

William loved his new job as head writer of a ghostwriting book firm; he could no longer fight fires after an incident. During the day, he worked and loved every moment of it, but at night, he worried over his future with Tracy, afraid that she might end up like the rest, or whether, like she said, she would be the one who didn't. The more he tried to ignore the warning of his late father, the more his mind kept troubling him to seek help.

He woke that morning deciding to travel to Ogun state. He would visit the forest where all his troubles began. Tracy came in time to see him packing his clothes.

'Are you travelling?' she asked.

'Yes I am. I need to visit my village – maybe I can find a solution to this evil upon me.'

'Babe,' she said in a serene voice.

She was doing it again, using that tone on him.

'I thought we talked about this?'

'I know, but I'm doing this for your sake. What if something bad happens to you? I'll never forgive myself.'

Tracy scoffed as William returned to arranging his clothes in his travel bag. 'You dreamt of a ghost that looked like your father, but it could have been anyone, it could have been anything. Ghosts don't even exist; nor can you believe anything one says.'

'How then do you explain the deaths that I have caused?' he asked.

'Unfortunate coincidence,' Tracy exclaimed and stood and wrapped her arm around William's neck. 'I will be the proof that those were all coincidence, especially now that we need you.'

William paused. 'We! Who is we?'

Tracy smiled and rubbed her stomach.

* * * *

Eight months had passed and not once had William had a nightmare of the witches, nor had he seen his father's ghost again. Tracy was right, William thought. Nothing was wrong. It was just his subconscious playing tricks with his dreams, or perhaps, it was a hologram he had seen. He was convinced.

They lived happily, some nights together in each other's arms, and other nights apart, but in each other's mind. William kept reiterating to Tracy how she was a blessing in his life, to have come at the time she did: when he had no hope, when all he thought about was dying, yet, despite those thoughts he had found love. It is amazing how one can find love in the place one least expects to. Nothing bothered William. His life became perfect. He had found a love that cast away his worries and fears.

On Monday morning, William got to work to meet a client in

need of ghostwriting services who specifically requested him. A good way to start a new week, he thought. He sat back as he heard the woman narrate what she wanted then he took notes. Every part of the story was tragic, and had a tragic ending. After she left, he went back to his notes, and realised it looked familiar, it was similar to the life he was living. The only difference was in the name and ethnicity of the characters. He was troubled all over again.

That same night, for the first time in a long time he dreamt. First it was the sisters mocking him and laughing, then they began to beckon him towards them. He struggled not to obey, and jerked up from his sleep. Scared, he turned to Tracy. She lay peacefully asleep beside him. He let out a sigh of relief. He lay back down to sleep, but fear had taken over his eyes, he could not close them.

At the break of first light, William woke Tracy from her sleep.

'Hey. Is everything okay?' asked Tracy wiping sleep from her eyes.

'Honey, can you please not go to work today?'

'Why?'

'Well you are getting very heavy for a start, and the weather looks threatening. I wouldn't want Junior to face the harsh sun.'

Tracy chuckled and lay back, whispering the name 'Junior' beneath her breath. 'Who names a child Junior anymore?' Tracy laughed.

William laughed too, but deep down berated himself for not telling her that his nightmares had returned and he was scared for her life and that of his unborn child. He didn't want her to think he was insecure.

* * * *

William hurried home as soon as the emergency call he had received about Tracy ended. He left work for home as fast as his legs and car could carry him, and on the way kept cursing himself and praying that whatever had happened to Tracy wasn't as grave as the voice of the caller. He got to the front of the house and saw people gathered. He ran past them, resisting their attempt to prevent him from entering his flat.

On the floor lay Tracy in a pool of her own blood. He fell on his knees and cried profusely.

'Don't drown another soul in your pool of death,' his father's voice echoed in his ear. He wished he had listened. He wished he hadn't listened to Tracy; now she was the victim of his negligence and disobedience.

He saw a letter on the centre table. It was a note from her husband in Port Harcourt. *She was married!* He mumbled in disbelief. She had run away from him and relocated to Lagos having stolen his money. The man had tracked her down and made her pay for her crime. The price was death.

William sat next to Tracy's body. The images of the bodies he had held in his arms began to flash before his eyes. He wept again. In between his tears, he lay beside her, closed his eyes, and hoped that they would never open again.

The three witch sisters in their fierceness appeared and surrounded him. This time, they didn't laugh, nor did they mock him; instead, their smiles were calm and gentle.

William felt a strong presence and opened his eyes.

'Why?' William asked with candour. There was nothing to fear anymore.

'It is time for you to join us,' Fire answered, sparkles of flame in her eyes. 'William Craig. You're not a man, you're a god, our husband, and you can love no one except us.'

'Why make me suffer for my father's sin?'

'You get it all wrong, our dear husband,' Rain responded, gentleness in her voice. 'You are your father's sin.'

'Take me,' William said and closed his eyes. 'I am all yours.'

Acknowledgement

Some stories in this book appeared in Decolonial Passage, The Brussels Review, Bandit Fiction, Random Photo Journal and an excerpt on my website. A warm-hearted thank you to the editors of these magazines. I must thank John Munro of Gorbals writing group. 'We are both alike because of our passion for writing,' he told me. 'I must have your book on my shelf before the year ends.' That book is here.

I must without fail thank Phoebe who is always the first eyes on my works; your time, comments and suggestions are precious to me as are you. If it wasn't for the constant reminder of your experience of how you missed a train stop and ended up in Liverpool, I probably wouldn't have been conscious during my first train travel in the UK and ended up missing my stop and finding myself in Liverpool too or worse. So yes, like you said, to which I agree, you are the beginning of the Diary of a Black Immigrant.

I appreciate Olusola Ali for reviewing the first set of stories in this collection. Your efforts can't be forgotten regardless of time.

A special mention to David Brudnybn and Colin Baron (aka Seán Batty) of Jist Misto for not making me lack food, for the countless humorous conversations about a lot of things, and for not making work seem like work.

Finally, to everyone who was directly or indirectly involved in the putting together of this book, I thank you.

ALBRIN JUNIOR is an award winning author, poet, scriptwriter, and director. His novel, *Naked Coin*, a historical fiction action thriller, was a runner up at the Akachi Ezeigbo prize for literature, and won the Lagos Book House Award for the Book of the year in 2020. Born in Lagos Nigeria, Albrin holds a BSc in Geography and Regional Planning from Ambrose Alli University and an MLitt in Creative Writing from the University of Glasgow, where he was also honoured with African Excellence Award. You can discover more about his journey at www.albrinjunior.com.